Noah

Into the
African Unknown

Noah

Into the
African Unknown

The further adventures of the mouse who could read

DOUGLAS FLOEN

ILLUSTRATIONS BY
KAITLYN SHAW

authorHOUSE®

AuthorHouse™ LLC
1663 Liberty Drive
Bloomington, IN 47403
www.authorhouse.com
Phone: 1-800-839-8640

Published by AuthorHouse   04/04/2014

ISBN: 978-1-4969-0270-2 (sc)
ISBN: 978-1-4969-0271-9 (e)

Library of Congress Control Number: 2014906211

DEDICATION

Dedicated to my wife Maureen without whose editing powers, criticisms, and constant encouragement this book would never have been written.

CHAPTER 1

Noah Hears From Gaia

NOAH AWOKE WITH A start; high above outside the barn where he slept in a cozy nest a raging storm was under way. He listened, alert as something out amidst the thunder and rush of rain was calling his name. He pushed himself up out of the warm duck feathers that lined his nest, left his sleeping grandpa and made his way up the sides of a crack that split the foundations of the barn. Creeping out onto the dark barn floor he could hear the sounds of storm and he felt himself drawn to the barn door that someone had left carelessly half open.

Sitting in the opening he watched as lightning flooded Wild Wold farmyard with blue white light. As he watched the rain pouring down, he listened for the sound that had awakened him. There it was again; it seemed to come from the wind now lashing the branches of the trees, from the raindrops pelting down and splattering in the pools of water forming in the barnyard. Most of all, it seemed to come from behind, above and all around.

Noah listened carefully as the sound rushed around him, "Noah, you are grown up now," whispered the voice. "You have been given a gift by Gaia the mother of all nature and the source of all life. Gaia is everywhere and watches over all and will protect you but you must honour the powers given to you and use them for the betterment and protection of nature. Go, Noah, out into the world and always, always remember that Gaia is the magic word."

The storm was passing, the thunder and echo and the flashing lightning distant. The world was silent and dark but for the drip, drip of drops from the leaves of the trees and a faint glow from the distant storm. After a while, Noah made his way back to his nest and spent the rest of the night in fitful and troubled sleep.

Noah's instructions from Gaia were that he was to use the powers that had been mysteriously given to him for the good of all nature. How he was to do this, he wasn't as yet quite sure. He had, however, been told by the rushing wind and the blowing rain that everything would take care of itself, and all would be revealed. Noah, being the kind of mouse he was, could not just relax and let nature guide him. He worried about this new responsibility and the next day found him sitting in the barn loft windows staring moodily out across the farm hoping for an inspiration. How he wished that Snoad, his barn cat friend, were here to give him advice or at least, to listen to him talk about his concerns. Snoad, however, was long gone, killed in an effort to save Noah's life.

Noah did not really have any close friends except for Dorcas, a lovely young mouse, with whom he had had several adventures. These adventures had lead to misfortune and trouble and so, Dorcas' father and mother kept a very close eye on their girl, making sure she was home after mouse school and doing her chores and homework. This left very little time for socializing with Noah, although they both would have liked to see each other more often.

This is a good time to mention that Noah and school did not get along well. The other young mice did not understand an odd one like Noah; he who would rather spend time on the farm garbage dump than learning mouse-life techniques from Madame Topal the very strict and unbending teacher, who ran the school with a paw of iron. Noah, although he wouldn't admit it even to himself was lonely and, though he was extremely self reliant and could find his own fun, he would have liked to share some of his adventures with someone else.

This thought brought him back to earth from his daydreaming. He was no longer a young mouse with nothing to do but laze away the days in Munificent Meadow. Now he needed to face up the responsibilities that he had been given by Gaia the night before. Not for him the life that was to be led by the other mice his age. They were to go to school, learn lessons in nest building and camouflage and avoidance of raptors, and while Noah knew that these were important life lessons, there was something that told him he was destined for other greater things. With all these heavy thoughts weighing him down, Noah felt restless he must do something, but what?

He listlessly left the barn and made his cautious way toward the garbage dump to check out the discarded papers, books and magazines that farmer Boaz' wife placed there when finished with them. Today there were no other mice or rats around searching through the garbage for bits of discarded food that might make a tasty meal and so, Noah was relieved to see that he had the place to himself. He was glad of this as, this way, he did not have to explain what he was doing for they just could not adjust to the sight of a mouse sitting reading a paper. They felt it went against all mouse-like behaviour and they often treated Noah with contempt or disdain. Today, the dump was clear of all others. Perhaps everyone stayed away, being such a sunny, clear day, it was easy for prowling cats, foxes or even hawks high in the sky to spot a mouse snack. Noah saw, to his joy, that Mrs. Boaz had, that same morning, discarded a fresh pile of her monthly subscription magazines.

He scurried quickly to the pile and began to nose among them to find what might be interesting. Among the pile of various homemaker and farm management magazines was one called *The Geographic*, and it was one of Noah's favourites, because it contained not only interesting stories about far off places but beautifully colored photos. Noah pushed the magazine under a leafy overhanging bough of a maple tree that had grown up in the centre of the garbage dump and, knowing he would not be seen there he settled down to do some reading.

The table of contents indicated that there were articles about animals in different parts of the world. Noah, who had a great curiosity about anything to do with the world, and particularly the world of nature, decided that he would first read about those wonderful large cats called cheetahs that live in southern Africa, a continent that Noah had read about and knew contained many large and small animals that were very different from those that he encountered around Wild Wold farm. He sat comfortably on the first page of the article and began to read. He was surprised to learn that cheetahs are the fastest animals in the entire world, and that they can achieve speeds of up to 65 miles an hour. They live by chasing down various kinds of prey such as zebra, antelope and waterbuck and they live in what is known as savannah, a dry, grass-covered land with scattered clumps of bushes and occasional rock outcrops, in which they would raise their three or four cubs.

Noah gazed at the pictures with great interest and, as he gazed and took in the entire scene, he remembered the time he had been with Snoad his cat friend, and he had been looking at pictures in a book and had concentrated so hard that his powerful imagination had drawn him into the picture. This was a gift that he had been given but he had had a bad experience that time, nearly being dropped into a boiling cauldron by three witches. He had not made use of his powers since then, so frightened had he been and, had it not been for Snoad, he would not be here now. But Snoad was not near to protect him. Since then, he had grown a lot and felt that he was old enough and wise enough to use his powers of imagination and to see for himself, what it would be like to "drop" into the picture and to take part in the action. As he concentrated on the picture of the cheetah racing across the plain in pursuit of an antelope, he felt a strange sensation running through his body. He felt himself being drawn into the surroundings; ever so slowly, the edges of the magazine's pages began to blur and expand. Reality began to fade and slowly, as he concentrated harder and harder, he began to feel himself being lifted up and transported into another space and time. He awoke to this new reality with a start, as he suddenly realized that he was no longer staring at the picture, but that he was in it! And that he was clinging with all his might to the fur on the back of the racing cheetah.

Chapter 2

Noah Meets Raina

NOAH HAD PUT HIMSELF not only into the picture but into the hunt itself. Clinging for dear life, he could faintly make out the brown grass of the savannah racing past, as the cheetah was in full pursuit now and the only thing that Noah could do or think about was to hang on and hope not to fall off.

The cheetah raced on, the antelope bounding this way and that, to try to throw its pursuer of his track. The cheetah lived up to its name as the fastest animal on earth by weaving in and out, following the antelope's crazed path without a pause or second's stop for breath. Finally the antelope made a fatal mistake and, upon coming to the bed of a dry stream it paused briefly, not knowing whether to jump or to swerve to the side. In that instant of indecision, the cheetah leapt a leap that took it from a flat out running chase to a sudden halt, landing upon the antelopes' back. The fear-crazed animal, its magnificent brown eyes bulging madly from its head, fell flat and the cheetah, like a well-oiled machine, placed both its paws upon its neck and holding on to its head with its fangs twisted sharply and broke it. The beast lay kicking and finally, its body quivering, it lay still.

Noah, who had certainly not reckoned on being a part of such a dramatic and dangerous experience, still clung, dazed, to the back of the cheetah, almost too frightened to allow himself to get down. And if he did get down, what then? The young mouse had little time to think. Things happened fast in the world of animals and the cheetah began immediately to squat over the dead body of the antelope and commence to tear into the stomach, as this is where the most rich and delicious parts of the animal can be found. Noah now slipped down the side of the cheetah onto the dry grass along side. He was somewhat dazed and shocked. He had, growing up as a wild animal on the farm, seen acts of violence and savagery, it is the way of nature, but he had never experienced firsthand such a violent display. He sat beside the hungry cat who was now devouring the antelope at great speed. Already, hyenas, those dog-like scavengers, and vultures, birds who flapped down from the cloudless sky, were hovering nearby, waiting for a chance to slip in and grab a piece of flesh or a morsel of entrails from under the watchful eyes of the watchful cheetah. The cat snarled and growled at these interlopers and whenever they came too close, she would turn and lash out at them, her tail switching wildly. They would have their fill much later when the cheetah had finished and gone back to her lair to feed her cubs.

Many times had Noah seen animals hunting and bringing down prey, but the foxes and birds that hunted near his home were nothing like the size of these animals. Noah remained where he was, not quite sure of what his next move should be. He knew instinctively, that he must not move too far from the large cat's side, as he would really be lost in a country he knew nothing about. And so, he remained huddled, hidden in the grass until the cheetah had eaten its fill.

At this point, the cat, which now began thinking about a waterhole to satisfy its thirst, turned a blood-stained face around and spotted Noah for the first time. The large animal blinked several times and looked as if it would pounce.

"What are you looking at, insignificant rodent whom I could polish-off with one snap of my powerful jaws . . . well, as they say, has the cat got your tongue?"

With this, the large cat, who had been speaking in Nature Natter, a language common to all animals, now broke off and began laughing at her own joke.

"I, I, just dropped in for a visit," stuttered Noah, realizing how lame and silly that sounded but could think of nothing else to say under the circumstances.

"If I weren't so full of dinner and so winded after that fast chase, I would have to see about you serving as a dessert."

Chuckling to herself, she got up from her crouched position over the half-eaten carcass of the antelopes and stretched to her full length in a luxurious stretching movement. She was now full and sleepy and no one knew she was the least dangerous in this mood. He now had an opportunity to take in this magnificent animal at perhaps closer quarters than was wise. She was a beautiful sight: long, lean with a thick, light-brown fur coat spotted with a wonderful pattern of darker brown spots. Her eyes were like glassy agate marbles and looking into them, Noah felt that he could see and understand all the mysteries of the wild. Her ears were surprisingly small, like tufts that stood up on either side of her intelligent face. The cheetah now lay down so that her head was inches away from Noah's tiny body.

Lazily, she blinked at him and in a low purring voice, she inquired, "I know that you are not from around here, mouse. For one thing, your markings are different from local mice. For another, your Nature Natter is hard to understand and finally, no local mouse would be so foolhardy as to sit, in the open, beside a feeding cat. Now, before I have you for dessert, tell me, just out of curiosity, just what are you doing here?"

Noah gulped hard; he realized that his story would have to be a good one, in order for him to hang on to his life.

"Well," he stuttered, "I can't really explain everything to you . . ." He was stalling for time now, trying to decide how much of his story a wild cat in the middle of the African Savannah would understand or believe. He kept hesitating, trying to find a reason beyond his own curiosity that had brought him to this strange place, so far from the safety and familiarity of home.

"Hurry, little rodent, your time is fleeting," purred the cat, now pushing a fraction nearer and yawning, so that Noah could see for himself those blood-stained fangs and that huge mouth that could swallow him in one fast gulp.

The cat moved a fraction closer to Noah, all the while regarding him from beneath half closed green eyes. Noah glanced about, but he could see nothing but tawny cat above and around him.

His ears then caught a whisper, a sighing sound that seemed to come from nearby that came, in his mind, from the earth below and from the cloudless sky above, even the leaves of the single nearby tree bent ever so slightly as they shivered in the slight zephyr of gentle wind. Earth was speaking to him again, Gaia was whispering instructions, and the things that he had been told in the storm that night were coming true. Gaia had told him he would be protected and that he had a mission. This was his reason for being here.

Summoning up his confidence, he stood up on his hind legs and looked the cat straight in the eye. "I was sent here by Gaia," he said bravely, now unafraid. "Yes, Gaia sent me to find out about how animals in other parts of the world live, and what can be done to help them survive in the world of man." Noah tried to look as large and confident as he could but it was a little difficult when up against such a huge animal as this.

"And just what can a miniscule mouse, such as yourself, do to save the animal world from extinction?" asked the now amused cat.

"Gaia has told me that everything will be revealed to me. Gaia has given me word that it is I who am to go out into the wild and see what can be done. She reasoned that such an insignificant being, such as myself, could go about and have access to places that a large and powerful animal, such as yourself, could not."

The cat seemed to mull this over for a time, all the while cleaning and grooming its face and paws. Finally, after what seemed a very long time to Noah, the cat sat up, stretched again and yawned once more.

"I want to hear more about this, mouse. What you have told me makes sense, but now I must return to my lair, as my two little ones are waiting for their evening meal and night is approaching."

Noah noticed now that the shadows were lengthening across the flat, prairie-like savannah.

"What I propose is this," said the cat, "if you will put your trust in me, I will treat you with respect, take you back to my lair and there you can meet my little cubs and tell me more about what Gaia said and what you are to do. I, of course, know of Gaia the mother of all Earth and nature, but I have never met anyone who has had instructions from her or even spoken to her. She is everywhere, in the earth, the sky, the very grass beneath my paws . . . Gaia is life itself and if you have a 'message' from her, then I should listen".

Noah could not help but notice the sudden change in this violent and savage animal. As soon as he had mentioned Gaia's name, the cat had relaxed its manner and become interested and concerned. It seemed that the word 'Gaia' was one that could command attention and soothe even the wildest of animals. Noah wondered at this power and began slowly to understand how he might move about and remain protected in this strange and hostile environment. He thought quickly and decided that this is what he must do: he must leave home for a period of time and follow whatever plans Gaia had for him. Not everything would be revealed at once and even now, he was unsure of just what good he could do for the animal world, but he understood that this was his mission, to follow wherever he was led, to obey his instincts and the messages in the wind.

"Yes," he answered in a new voice, one of assuredness, "I will trust you and be glad to come with you to your lair, meet your young ones and talk further with you."

"Good," replied the cat, "Hop on my back and away we'll go."

Noah did as he was asked, climbing up the thick, course fur of the cat's side until he was safely seated between the animal's ears. This was just how he used to ride with Snoad his old friend, but the cat had been much smaller than this one and so, the view that Noah now got was, because he was so much higher up, quite spectacular for a tiny mouse that seldom saw above the grass at ground level.

All around him, the vast plains stretched off until the edge of the sky, the brown and yellow of the dried out grasses melted in the far distance into a deep indigo color of the horizon heralding the approaching evening. Here and there were stunted, twisted trees, their branches reaching skyward in the weirdest fashion, almost as if they were trying to climb the ladderless sky to escape the heat and dryness below. Outcroppings of black rock dotted the plain and it

9

was in the shadow of one of these that the cheetah, after trotting for some distance, kept her lair, a dug out shallow depression under the protecting overhang of rock.

The outcrop was situated on a slight rise of land and Noah, as they came closer, realized that the cheetah could survey from miles around from the top of the outcrop, which gave her an advantage when it came to spotting prey or the nearness of any enemies. As they came near, Noah could make out the faint, hungry cries of the baby cheetahs. At the mouth of her home, the cheetah stopped and answered these cries with a soft growl of her own that instantly silenced them.

"Here we are," said the cat, "I will go on in ahead to settle them down and warn them that you are a guest and must be treated gently. My little ones are lively and might mistake you for a toy to be played with," she hesitated, "or worse". With that, she disappeared down the slight incline to her cave and Noah, who sat at the cave's mouth, now could hear the squeals and mewling of the excited baby cheetahs.

The mother reappeared and said kindly, "If you don't mind waiting, I will feed my little darlings and then they'll sleep and we will talk. If you are hungry, there are grasses over there that have seeds that you might like, go, feed yourself and we will discuss later".

Noah now realized that he was very hungry and began foraging in the thick grasses that grew not far away. There he found seeds of different varieties than he was used to back at the farm; however he liked their taste and devoured enough to fill himself. As he was thirsty, he discovered that, now evening had arrived, dew had formed on the undersides of the grasses so he satisfied his thirst by licking this liquid gift.

The cheetah had come to the mouth of her lair and now called softly for Noah to enter and meet her young, who were full of their mother's milk and were cuddling down for their night's sleep. Noah ventured into the dark opening; he had begun to lose the fear that he had had earlier. He knew that, at any moment, the cheetah could snatch him up and crush him in those frighteningly powerful jaws, but the mention of the word 'Gaia' seemed to pacify her and turn her into a quiet and thoughtful being.

Inside the dim cave, Noah could make out two tiny baby cheetahs, their fur soft and downy, a whitish color covered with the darker spots that would change again, as they grew older and developed their adult coat.

"My name is Raina," spoke the cheetah in a low growling purr, "and these are my little ones. Aren't they wonderful to see?"

Noah had to agree, the young ones hardly looked fierce at all, but rather soft and gentle in their slumber. It was obvious that Raina was extraordinarily proud of them.

"Let us go and sit where we can watch the sunset. There we can talk and you can tell me what Gaia has told you and what you intend to do about it".

And so, the two rather oddly matched animals sat side by side, the one towering over the other, as the sun began its descent into the far distant horizon. The colors were an explosion of reds, purples and oranges, as the sun sank behind layers of low-laying clouds. So this was Africa, thought Noah, as the two sat silently watching the beautiful gift of nature, and it was at this twilight moment that an odd, useful and devoted friendship began to grow and take shape.

CHAPTER 3

A Friendship Begins

R AINA AND NOAH SAT long into the African night with its strange and, to Noah's unaccustomed ears, sometimes frightening noises. From far off came the blast of an elephant, trumpeting the herd to the waterhole. Later the cough of a prowling leopard, as it stalked some unsuspecting prey. Night on the African Savannah brought with it the appearance of many animals that slept or kept hidden during the day. Noah and Raina talked and talked, Noah told of life on a farm and Raina of life on the African plains. She spoke of the various animals that lived there, the lions, rhinos, antelope, monkeys, crocodiles and many more. As she spoke of them, her sadness grew and to Noah's complete surprise, this fierce animal broke down into tears.

"What is wrong?" asked Noah softly. He was sensitive to the feelings of others and did not want to embarrass this magnificent animal.

"Nothing, just a momentary lapse that's all," replied Raina, trying to regain her dignity. A silence followed, but then Raina turned to Noah and said in a voice full of passion and emotion, "It's not just my little ones I worry about, but all of nature's folk who live here, we are all in terrible danger and it gets worse. With every passing year, more and more of us disappear; we are caught in cruel traps, shot at, poisoned or herded into pits. Someday, there will be not one of us left to wander the wild, as we have done since time began."

This outburst was followed by an even longer silence, finally broken again by Raina who said quietly, "Why burden you with this, Gaia may have sent you here but what really can one of your size do against the men who trap, kill and drive us from our natural homes?"

Again silence as Noah digested all of this and finally said, "I think Gaia knew what to do in sending me here. Yes, I am small and insignificant compared to you and many other savannah folk, but I do have several powers that might be put to good use". And with this, Noah began to tell Raina about his ability to understand human writing and language.

Raina listened carefully; she was beginning to realize that this tiny mouse was a true powerhouse of a different sort than she was used to, and that his gifts might prove helpful.

"I believe that I was sent here for a purpose and that our meeting here today was not an accident but part of a greater plan, one that we perhaps do not know entirely just yet but a plan that is to benefit everyone on the savannah."

The two animals continued to talk far into the night, Raina telling stories of the poachers, groups of cruel and unfeeling men who trapped certain animals such as the rhinoceros and cut off their horns as they lay dying.

"What do they want with their horns?" asked Noah.

"I believe that they make a powder of them and sell it to people in far off Asia who think that they have magical properties," said Raina, "and slowly the rhino is disappearing. Soon there will be none left, as with the herds of elephants that they hunt and kill just for their tusks, which humans prize for jewellery and ornaments." Raina went on, "Then, if it isn't the poachers, it is groups of men who come to capture babies such as mine or even grown animals to take to far-off places to be penned up in zoos for humans to come and look at. All of this is wrong and we are powerless to stop it. Oh yes, I could attack any one of those men but what would be the use? They have guns and poison and if something happened to me, how would my little ones survive? They would starve to death and the men would skin me to make a coat for some lady in a far-off city."

There was a thoughtful silence for a while, as Noah digested these terrible facts. Raina broke the silence by saying, "But it's late now, we must get some sleep. I won't hunt tomorrow but rather, I will take you about to meet some of the others who live in this area. I'll be your guide and protector if you like." Noah was very tired and thought this a good idea.

Raina said, "It would be best if you curled up in my den. Passing snakes, who have not met you, might just see you as a quick snack."

And so, the two disappeared into the den, where Raina curled up protectively around her litter and Noah found a comfortable and warm spot nearby. Soon all was silent as the cheetah and the mouse slept soundly, each dreaming dreams of men with guns and traps coming for them and cruel, yawning pits waiting to swallow them up.

CHAPTER 4

Noah Meets Africa

THE NEXT MORNING, NOAH woke very early to the harmony of many different birds chorusing. Their song filled the air and Noah was again stuck with the great differences between his home and this new one in sights, sounds and smells. He looked around and saw that Raina had already left the cave and the two cubs were side by side in a corner silently staring at him. He made an attempt to approach them but, at a movement from him, they sank back into the corner and spat and hissed. He realized that they had never been outside the cave before and to them, he was an interloper, an alien being, and although their mother had told them that he was a guest and should be treated gently, they were still shy and unsure.

Noah scurried out of the cave and sat on the edge of the outcrop gazing off into the distance which stretched on as far as the eye could see. Below him on the plain, a morning haze was beginning to clear off and Noah could see huge herds of various kinds of cloven-hoofed animals such as antelope, gnus, zebra and gazelles. These herds moved and fed from the grasses that grew there. Noah didn't know this as yet, but nature had provided these animals in their multitudes as food for the much smaller population of larger animals such as lions, cheetahs, etc. The natural balance seems cruel and uncaring. Death is a constant threat, but it is the way of life and everyone in Gaia's world accepts this as natural. Raina now appeared and it was obvious from the traces of blood on her mouth that she had been at the remains of yesterday's antelope kill.

"Good morning, young mouse, have you managed to sleep well and find some breakfast?" said she, and Noah could tell from the friendly tone of her voice that she had accepted him as a friend and that he need not worry any longer about serving as a small lunch for this magnificent, but fearsome, animal.

"Good morning yourself," replied the mouse, "I have found seeds that were very tasty, thank you."

"Good, and have you met my babies?"

"Yes, I have, but they were very shy and did not let me get too close to them."

"They are shy, they have not been out of their home as yet and have never met anyone from the animal world, but when they get to know you, I am sure that you will find them as delightful as I do."

Noah nodded and smiled to himself, thinking that all mothers are the same, large and small around the world. Noah had never known a mother's love, as his own mother had been swept away in a flood when he was very young and he felt a little envious of the two tiny cheetahs.

"If you are ready, then perhaps we could go out onto the savannah and meet other folk who live hereabouts and you could listen to their stories. I assure you, you will have nothing to fear, as long as you are with me and as long as you mention that Gaia has sent you to us."

"I'm ready anytime you are," replied Noah, now feeling sure of himself and confident that he was under protection and had a purpose to fulfill.

"Well, just let me check on my little ones and then we'll be off." Raina disappeared into her lair and Noah could hear soft snuffling and purrs, as she caressed her cubs and made sure they were safe and comfortable. When she reappeared, Noah climbed up the fur of her shoulder and settled between her ears.

Off this odd couple went, travelling slowly down the rocky outcrop and out onto the vast plain that was dotted with herds of grazing animals. The various antelope, zebra and gazelles looked up from their munching of dried grasses but, while they kept a wary eye on the strolling cheetah, they seemed to know instinctively that, this morning, their mortal enemy had something else on her mind than attacking one of them. Raina took her time, seemingly disinterested in the herds of prey that were within reach of her lightening like ability to outrun even the fastest gazelle.

"I'm looking for a friend of mine," she explained to Noah over her shoulder. "She can usually be found near that clump of bushes, she too has a little one and at this time, she is very shy and protective of her young. They are quite helpless for a long time and she doesn't give birth or hide in a lair like mine."

The two approached a thick clump of bushes and it was here that Noah made the acquaintance of Sheba, the rhinoceros. Noah was startled upon first catching site of this gigantic animal that was hidden deep inside the cover of gray-green, low-lying bushes. She was perfectly camouflaged and Noah thought immediately of all of those lessons taught by Madame Topal back at mouse school about the importance of camouflage as a protection against predators. How this animal needed protection, Noah didn't understand at first, as she was huge and was covered with a thick hide that not much could pierce. Not only was she covered with this protective outer armour, but at the end of her blunt nose, projected a single huge horn that, Noah imagined, could deal out a great deal of harm to anyone unfortunate enough to find themselves at the other end of it. Huge thick legs supported her tremendous bulk with a short, busy tail at the end of her body. This tank-like beast looked up from where she had been tending her small offspring, which was a miniature version of herself. Immediately, she was on guard, moving protectively in front of her young and looking as if she would charge at any moment. Her massive head swung from side to side as she snorted angrily and began to paw the earth beneath her hoofs.

"Relax Sheba, it is only me, Raina," called out the cheetah in a reassuring voice. "I'm sorry to disturb you when you are with your young one, but I have a small friend that I want you to meet."

Sheba stopped pawing the earth and warily regarded the cheetah from tiny, near-sighted eyes.

"Is that you Raina? What are you doing here and why are you disturbing me when I'm with my little one? I could have charged you and put an end to you forever you know."

Raina laughed rather nervously, "I could outrun you any day and you know it."

"Well, be that as it may, what brings you so far from your own lair? Shouldn't you be out running down some antelope for your dinner?"

"I did that yesterday, and so I don't need to hunt for several days," replied Raina. "As I said, I have brought you someone quite interesting to meet. He has come from far off and I think you should relax and get to know him."

With that she hunched down beside the massive head of the rhino so that Noah, on her shoulder, was within view of this animal that for all her power could only see short distances. She now peered dimly at Noah and when she was able to make him out, she backed up snorting with indignation and turned, herding the little one as if to leave.

"Is this some sort of a joke that you think is funny, disturbing me and my young one with a silly insignificant mouse, which I could get rid of in an instant with one stamp of my hoof? Are you crazy, do you have nothing better to do than run about the countryside with a mouse as a partner? Really, I think you have quite lost your mind. I hope word of this doesn't get out, you'll be the laughing stock of the whole area. Are you so lonely that you must take up with miserable rodents? How will you explain this to your young when they are old enough to understand their mother's shame?"

Raina listened to this torrent from her friend with patience and finally said in a calm voice, "If you are quite finished with what you think, perhaps you will listen while I explain. I met my new friend here last evening, his name is Noah and he is from far away, and while he speaks Nature Natter as all animals do, his accent is quite different and as you can see, his markings are not the same as the mice that we see hereabout. He has come with protection from Gaia."

18

Before Raina could continue, Sheba interrupted, saying, "Why didn't you say in the first place that Gaia had something to do with this?"

"You hardly gave me a chance," replied Raina dryly. "His name is Noah and he has powers such as we have never encountered here in the animal world. He can read and speak human language. Isn't it something?" she finished up proudly.

"Humph, I don't see what is so wonderful about anything that has to do with cursed humans. I spend my days and nights worrying and wondering how to keep them from stealing my baby or killing me for my horn. They are everywhere and my people are becoming rarer and fewer, as are yours, Raina, and as are the elephants and many other of the folk who try to make a home here."

Noah listened carefully to what was being said and finally, he spoke up and said, "I think I see the problem."

"The problem?" snorted the rhino. "Do you have enough time to hear all the problems that we have? If it isn't poachers, then it's herders, farmers, hunters or zoo keepers all wanting to skin us, eat us, sell us, or just plain kill us for the fun of it. We have no resources; we have absolutely no way of defending ourselves against guns, traps and poison. I could charge any one of those humans in an open combat and I know that, with my superior strength and speed, I could knock them sideways into tomorrow, but they never come out into the open to fight. No, they lay their traps at night or come in those metal moving machines that I can ram and ram but never overcome. They have all the advantages, and so we just have to spend our days hiding, instead of walking about in the open like the powerful animals we are." She finished up with a snort and shifted her heavy body about and, without a further word, herded her little one into an even denser part of the covering bush.

"We had better not bother her any more," said Raina, "she is very short tempered and if we provoke her, she could lose it and that could be disastrous."

Noah sat on the shoulder of the cheetah and thought of the time that Munificent Meadow had almost been turned into a shopping mall by greedy humans who thought nothing of the needs or lives of the natural folk who lived there. That time, he had used his abilities to read and formed a plan that made use of all the inhabitants of the meadow. It had been successful, but this problem seemed beyond him. How could he gather together all the animals of the African plain and make any kind of resistance to this danger that did not just come from one source but from many?

Raina now began to arise to leave the bushes and, as she did so, she said to Noah, "The day is still young, let's walk about and see if we can meet anyone else, perhaps we will be lucky enough to find Zola and her family of elephants. They usually can be found wherever there is shade to protect them from the fierce heat of the day."

Noah had noticed the heat. He was not used to it, coming from a northern climate, but as the cheetah loped along, her long, lithe body moving a steady pace, a slight breeze kept Noah cool, sitting between her ears. Past a group of warthogs, who lifted their ugly heads with their dangerous tusks and watched warily as Raina trotted by but, when they saw that she had other things on her mind than prey this day, they went back to feeding, snorting and grunting as they did so. Passed herds of various animals that would pause in their grazing to watch and see if Raina posed a danger or not, and then going back to contentedly cropping the rich, dry grasses. Noah began to understand that, while these animals were preyed upon and suffered terrible fates; this was the way of the plain. These animals existed in their thousands, in order to provide food for the few such as Raina, the prides of lions or the occasional leopard and that, when they knew that any one of these predators was full of food and had provided for their offspring, they did not pose a danger and could be ignored with safety.

Raina and Noah had travelled quite a distance from Raina's lair and, as they came nearer to a line of trees that bordered the river, Raina said, "If we can't find Zola here, I will want to return to my little ones. I can't travel too far from them without checking to make sure of their safety, what with poachers and zoo people prowling about, one has to be constantly vigilant."

As they approached the line of trees, Noah could hear a strange confusion of sounds: weird trumpeting, rumbles, grunts, screams, and splashing.

"We are in luck, the local herd is here at their watering and bathing place," said Raina.

As they made their way through the trees, the noises became louder and even more confusing, and when they came upon the bank of the narrow stream, a sight met Noah's eyes that frightened and, at the same time, fascinated him. There on the muddy shore and out into the middle, were these magnificent, gigantic grey-coloured beasts. They were having the time of their lives apparently, wallowing in the sloppy, mud-coloured water, on their sides, gurgling as they sucked water into their long, snake-like trunks and sprayed it out onto their backs, swimming, wading and just enjoying every minute. The river, which had once been wide, had shrunk, as the hot weather had evaporated much of it and the streams feeding it had dried up, leaving a narrow ribbon of water for animals to drink from and, in the case of the elephants, to use as a swimming hole.

Noah, who although very clean about himself had never seen animals frolic and enjoy mud and water so much. His friend Giles, the otter, back at the farm loved and played in the water but that water was clear and running. This water was partly mud, but that didn't seem to spoil these huge animals' enjoyment of it.

"Let's wait until they have finished and all come ashore," advised Raina. "It isn't wise to interrupt wild folk when they are about some action of their lives. An angry elephant after me is not a situation I would want to be in."

And so the two sat, hidden by some shrubs and watched as the herd finished up their bath and, one by one, returned to shore still trumpeting and bellowing and, by now, a yellowish-brown colour from the mud drying on their sides.

"Don't they want to wash off that mud?" asked Noah.

"No, it serves as a very useful purpose; it protects their skin from the sun and it protects them from insect bites, as you can see, they don't have the covering of fur as we do."

By this time, the last of the elephants had left the water and were gathered about an ancient female who seemed to be the leader of the herd.

"That's Zola and she is the head elephant, she leads the herd and decides what and when they do anything. I will move closer to her and signal that I am here in peace. There are several baby elephants and the herd will surround them to protect them from any danger."

Indeed, now Noah noticed that there were at least three very miniature versions of the larger animals, they too were covered in mud and they kept very close to the sides of their mothers. As Raina slowly left the cover of the bushes, the leader of the herd lifted her trunk high to scent the air, as she caught the smell of another animal. Upon catching sight of Raina, Zola lifted the sail-like flaps of her ears and trumpeted warningly. Raina quickly walked out into the open and said in a carrying voice:

"It is I, Raina the cheetah, and I come in peace. Let the blessings of Gaia be upon you. I have brought a small friend who has come from afar to meet us and get to know us of the savannah."

The elephant slowly let her ears flap down to lie beside her massive head, lowered her trunk and, in a softer voice, asked, "And who is this small friend you speak of?" I can see no one."

"He is right here, between my ears, can't you see him?"

The elephant moved closer, her trunk reaching out to sniff the air and to make out another presence and, once catching Noah's scent and finally seeing him crouched between Raina's ears, she backed off, her ears flapping out and her trunk high in the air, "Is this a joke, Raina? Do you not realize that we elephants have a mortal dread of mice? They are so tiny that we can't keep track of them and, if they run up inside of our trunk, they could cause us to suffocate and die!" With this screamed response, she trumpeted loudly and signalled the herd to move off.

"Wait!" called Raina. "This isn't a mouse as any other. He won't do anything to harm you; he has come in peace from Gaia."

With the mention of Gaia, Zola lowered her trunk and let her ears again fall to the side of her head.

"Well, if what you say is true, what is it he wants with us? Does he not realize that if he trifles with my people we could smash him out of sight with one stamp of our foot?"

"I'm sure that he will be respectful of you in every way. I'm sure that he will keep his distance, so that you can see him at all times," purred Raina in as reassuring a manner as she could.

"In that case, let him come forward and speak to us and let him keep within my sight at all times," said Zola softening her deep rumbling voice as she did so.

Noah, who was learning that the magic word, 'Gaia', could soothe the most savage heart, stood up as tall as he possibly could and, from between Raina's ears said, "Hello, my name is Noah and I am here to get to know all of you here on the savannah. Gaia has spoken to me and has told me to talk to you of your troubles and she asked me to help if I can."

This was spoken bravely, and it flashed through Noah's mind the sight that this must be and, if any of the mice that he knew at home could see him now, they would be very impressed with his bravery, or think him an utter fool to have put himself in such a position.

His quick thought soon disappeared when the elephant, with a deep trumpeting gargle, laughed and said, "You expect me to believe that you could possibly be of any help to anyone except to make them laugh at your puny tininess? I'm sure that Gaia would have sent someone of strength and size to help us in our troubles."

"Well," replied Noah, "that may be, but I am here and I would like to get to know you better."

At this point Raina became rather agitated and spoke up saying, "I must get back to my little ones, daylight will be fading soon and I am farther from home than usual, so I must be off. Are you going to stay here with Zola's herd or are you coming with me, back to the lair?"

Before Noah could answer, Zola, to everyone's great surprise, suddenly said, "Let him stay here with me, he can sit half way up my trunk, where I can keep an eye on him and we can talk. I am really quite interested to hear what a mouse, who says he is asked by Gaia to come and meet us, has to say, and it better be good, as I don't usually waste my time with tiny folk except to chase them out of the way."

And so, much to Raina's surprise and delight, because she had persuaded the usually very shy and suspicious Zola to accept her word that Noah would not present any danger and would be interesting to talk to, Zola allowed this tiny mouse to scurry halfway up her trunk and perch there, as if it were the most natural thing in the world.

CHAPTER 5

A Night-time Tragedy

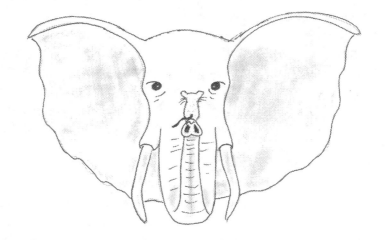

NOAH HIMSELF WAS RATHER proud that he seemed to be making friends with these giants of the animal world, but he was wise enough not to let it go to his head and so he kept his attention focused on where he was and with whom. He realized that any misstep on his part could put him in mortal danger.

Raina now said her goodbyes and sprinted off in the direction of the open plain and her home. Over her shoulder, she shouted to Noah, "Be sure to find me again and we will sit and talk some more."

Noah squeaked out his agreement, but his voice was probably lost in the midst of a herd of noisy elephants; there is a huge difference between the bark of a cheetah and the squeak of a tiny mouse.

Now Zola trumpeted her herd that it was time to leave the river bank, and make off toward their evening feeding grounds. Usually this herd was content to graze in amongst the grasses and shrubs that lived on the savannah, but the area that they grazed in was shrinking, because more humans were taking over their ancestral lands and cultivating them or fencing them off, in order to graze their cattle and goats. Because of this, Zola felt that her herd had the right to help itself to anything growing on what had once been their own land. This was true of the predators such as the lions, leopards and cheetahs; their instincts that guided them saw nothing at all wrong in jumping over or smashing down fences to feed on whatever they found there, this land had been theirs from the beginning of time and now Man was taking it over unasked and defending it with guns, traps and poison without any concern or care for the rights of those whose home it was.

Thus, Zola's instincts told her to head for an area that she knew used to have some very choice vegetation for her herd to eat. With Noah balancing, as best he could, on the waving trunk, Zola led the herd out onto the open plain. What a magnificent sight they made: the setting sun in a blaze of fiery colour and these beasts, whose ancestors had inhabited this plain since the dawn of time, marching single file behind their lead mother who kept a constant lookout for any danger.

By the time they reached their destination, a new farm that had only been fenced off in the last year, the sun had disappeared over the horizon and an inky blackness had descended. Noah did not let the darkness worry him as he knew that most animals could operate quite well in the dark; their eyes had an ability to gather every bit of light available and make their way through the darkest of nights.

When the herd came to the fence, they barely stopped their forward march. This was their ancestral land and they were going to treat it as they always had, a source of food. The gigantic beasts just trampled the fence, as though it were made of matchsticks. Over the fallen fence they marched, through the carefully ploughed fields and finally stopping at a crop of green and very tender shoots of grain. The herd began to pull out the plants by their roots with their trunks and stuffed the tasty greens into their mouths. Noah found it harder and harder to keep his balance on the ever busy trunk of Zola and so he said with his loudest voice, "Could you please set me down over there on that fencepost until you are finished, and then pick me up? I'm afraid I'll fall off your trunk and get trampled."

Zola agreed and very carefully curled her trunk around Noah's tiny body and, with great care, lifted him up and deposited him.

"There you can remain until we have finished, and then I'll come for you and pick you up again so that we can talk later while the herd is resting."

The herd continued feeding, not caring or understanding that their massive bulk was ungainly in a planned field and that with their huge hoofs, they were destroying as much as they were eating. Their natures were such that they would never understand the organized ways of man; they knew only that here was available food for them. They were not conscious of any desire to wreck the farmer's carefully tilled field, they were only responding to the needs that guided them.

The elephants had about eaten their fill and were waiting for a signal from Zola to lead them back to their resting place for the night, when a tremendous noise broke out. The elephants became wild-eyed and confused, swinging their heads from side to side to try and discover the source of this intrusion.

Mothers moved protectively to shield their young from whatever danger this might be. The source of the loud noises soon became apparent. Men with flaming torches, banging metal shields and firing volleys of rifle shots into the air were running about and surrounding the herd.

Zola trumpeted for calm but the confusion and fear were so great that the elephants panicked, their ears flapping and their trunks waving frantically in the air. They could see no way out and so, in their fear, they stampeded, trampling everything before them in a headlong rush to get away from this awful noise and the frightening sight of waving, flaming torches. These torches were being swung in wide arcs in the air, trailing streams of fiery sparks that landed on the tender hides of many of the herd and increased their panic and fear. They fled in disorder, the mothers vainly trying to guide and protect their young. The herd stampeded off, scattering in several directions and running until they reached the safety of the line of trees that they had left that afternoon. There, Zola reassembled the herd and imposed some sense of order.

The herd cowered in fear, these magnificent and stately animals vanquished by a small group of men intent upon saving their carefully tilled and seeded land. Who was to blame? As the herd reassembled, one mother trumpeted in despair, she could not find her newborn baby.

The herd all took up the lament and, as dawn was now breaking, they began to return to the fields that they had left so suddenly from the night before. They were looking for the lost baby and they milled about the now vacant field, snuffling and trumpeting their frustration and loss.

Finally, one of the herd found the tiny calf, it had become separated from its mother in the confusion and had been shot through the head. It laid, a tiny scrap of helpless, gray flesh, in a corner of the field. The mother stood over it, trying to get it to rise up. Again and again, she tried but it was of no use. Zola knew that they must leave this place of horror and she tried to coax the mother to leave the side of her dead baby, but the mother would not budge. Finally, Zola trumpeted the signal for the herd to leave and the mother reluctantly and slowly moved off to join the others, who then spent the remainder of the day huddled in the protective shade of the river tree line.

And what of Noah who had been gently placed on a fencepost just before the arrival of the men? He was a silent and horrified witness to the whole terrible night, he crouched down, thankful for his small size and watched as the elephants stumbled and ran off from the men and their torches. He saw the tiny elephant fall from a rifle bullet but he remained where he was, huddled down until the dawn brought back the grieving herd.

In her confusion and grief for the lost baby, Zola had completely forgotten about the tiny mouse who had ridden on her trunk, wishing to have a long talk with her. It wasn't until much later that day that she remembered but by then, it was too late to find him, wherever he might be. Noah watched as the elephants left the dead baby slowly. He knew that this was not the time to make his presence known. In their anger and grief, the herd might just turn their hostility upon him and so, he reluctantly climbed down from the fencepost and, after eating some grass seed, he sat and tried to figure out just what to do next.

He was not in a very good situation; he was miles from the cheetah's lair and wouldn't know how to get there in any case. He had lost contact with his only other acquaintance, the elephant, and now here he was hidden in the grass, not knowing where to go or to whom to turn. Noah was a very resourceful mouse, and usually he could figure his way out of any tight spot. If he went out onto the plain, he might encounter any number of strange and hostile animals that might just swallow him first, before he could mention Gaia, and ask questions afterwards.

27

CHAPTER 6

Bengo and Duma

As Noah sat huddled in the grasses pondering his next move, his ever sharp ears caught a rustling that came from nearby. Noah sat up, or rather, stood up on his hind legs and, his whiskers twitching, he surveyed as much of his surroundings as he could. His very sharp eyes caught a glimpse of a long, uncoiled snake gliding through the trampled remains of the field. It was on a hunt for worms and other insects that had been disturbed by the trampling elephants.

Noah's first thought was to run, and run fast. Snakes are amongst mice's worst enemies and Noah had no reason to believe that African snakes would be any different. As Noah prepared to scurry away to safety, a sudden thought came to him. Perhaps if he were to shout Gaia's name, it might have the same effect on the hunting snake, as it had had on the other animals that he had met so far in his visit to Africa.

And so, taking a deep breath and hoping for success, Noah climbed back up the fencepost and, from the top he stood right up in plain view and shouted, "Gaia, Gaia, Gaia," over and over again. To his surprise, and confusion, the snake below glanced up, muttered something like, "silly mice" and slithered off in the opposite direction, leaving a rather bewildered Noah.

His bewilderment did not last long, however, because others had heard his call and had come to investigate. A small animal had appeared from out of the grass and now crouched below the fence post looking up expectantly at Noah and, at the same time, a flutter of wings brought a strange looking bird to perch on a fallen fence rail.

The two very different animals spoke at once: "Who are you and why are you calling Gaia's name over and over?"

Looking down, Noah could make out the strangest animal he had ever encountered, it was covered with plate-like scales of a golden brown color and its body was a long shoulderless mass of these scales from its pointed, long nose to its scaly, long tail. It was not a reptile but certainly had the appearance of one. It had four scaly feet and as it moved, its tail switched back and forth. Its front paws were wide and ungainly-looking and as Noah watched in fascination, these paws scraped the moist earth uncovering many scurrying ants, which the animal lapped up with a long pointed tongue that flickered in and out of its mouth, carrying ants stuck to it into its open jaws. The bird that had spoken in response to Noah's call of Gaia was now down beside the strange animal pecking up any of the insects that escaped the busy tongue.

"I'm Noah and I am a friend of Gaia and I've come here to meet you and find out about your lives."

"Well, our lives are not what they used to be," snorted the armoured animal. "Everyday I have to thank Gaia for another day of life."

"Why is that?" asked Noah.

"Because, I am hunted day and night for my skin which is used to make shoes and handbags for the very wealthy in far off cities, and my skin is also used for medicines and some people even cut up my body and eat me . . . Isn't that reason enough to be grumpy about life? There are now so few of us left that I cannot find a mate to provide me with young, so that our species will not completely die out in a short time."

"That's terrible," said Noah, "can anything be done?"

"Nothing, as it is I've got to grab a quick meal here and then get to my nest and hide away from poachers who regularly raid this area hunting for me and others, so that they can sell us for food or for the parts of us that humans think they need or want."

Noah was learning fast that humans were the enemy and showed no care or concern for the animals whose home this was.

"What is your name, mine is Noah," stated the mouse in a friendly fashion.

"My name is Bengo and I am a pangolin and my people have inhabited these parts since time began. My friend here is Duma, the Hoopoe bird, and together we feed from ant and termite nests. That way we help keep the population of those insects down, so that they won't unbalance the nature. Now it is your turn, tell us about yourself.

Noah now proceeded to tell the two a little about his life, leaving out the information about his ability to understand and read human language. He felt, wisely, that it might confuse and lead to misunderstanding and mistrust if he allowed this information to be public. The mouse turned his attention to the bird that was also very odd looking, when compared to the birds Noah had known at home. This yellow and brown striped bird had a feather crest that stood straight up when the bird was excited or alert for danger. It had a long curved bill that was useful for pecking up ants and termites that escaped from the pangolin's busy tongue. Noah marvelled at how the two worked together without anger or selfishness.

Duma cackled and said, "Not all animals you will meet around here will get along as well as we do; we need each other, so we cooperate. I spot ants and termites and the ones he misses, I pick up. My family does not have the same problems that Bengo does. We can fly and that protects us somewhat from the poachers and others who would harm us."

During this conversation, Noah had crawled down from the fencepost and now sat on the trampled grass in front of his two new acquaintances. He knew instinctively that he had nothing to fear form these two, as they were not animals that preyed upon mice. He now related the sad story of the previous night and the three made their way to where the body of the baby elephant lay.

By this time, the carcass of the little animal had been partially devoured by several dog-like animals with vicious teeth and snarling expressions.

"Those are hyenas," whispered Bengo the pangolin. "Don't go near them when they are feeding and don't be shocked at what they are doing. They are nature's clean-up crew and they perform a valuable service.

"Valuable service! How?" questioned Noah.

But before Bengo could answer, Noah's own intelligence answered his question. "Oh, I think I get it," he said, "they clean up any fallen animals, so that the land is left tidy and neat."

"Yes, and what they can't eat, vultures come and finish up and after the vultures come, tiny insects that clean out even the hardest to get to corners of the dead animal do their part, so that, in a week or so, absolutely nothing is left but bones."

When Noah thought about it he knew that, more or less, the same thing went on at home, the only difference being that, at home, the animals seemed much smaller and not as colourful as the cheetah or as magnificent as the elephants. The same rules of nature seemed to apply wherever one found themselves.

Noah spent some more time chatting with his two new friends, he told them his life story or what he thought they should know and they quite freely told him about their life on the African savannah.

As evening seemed near, Noah sighed and said, "I really don't know where to go to spend the evening, could either of you tell me of a safe and comfortable place for me to sleep tonight?"

"That's easy," replied Duma, the hoopoe, "you can come with me. I'll let you ride on my back and take you back to my nest. I have four eggs that are being sat upon by Mrs. Hoopoe right now, but I'm sure that she will welcome you when she hears that you are from Gaia. Anyway," continued the brightly colored bird, "you wouldn't want to spend a night in Bengo's lair, it smells badly and is all of dirt."

Bengo reacted to this insult, he said, quite heatedly, "Can I help it if I was disturbed in my sleep the other night and, to protect myself from intruders, I had to use my scent glands, which, to everyone who comes near, gives of a terrible odour, and that odour keeps animals and humans away. So there, to you and your clean, tidy nest! You are lucky enough to build it in a tree."

"So what? You think I don't have trouble with predators there? How about the bands of monkeys that come rolling through the treetops, ready to snatch up my eggs or even a tiny hatchling if they so fancy, and how about tree snakes who slither up and down the trunk silently?"

By this time, the hoopoe was getting himself worked up, his crest standing upright and his feathers ruffled.

"Calm down, calm down," soothed the pangolin. "I know you have your problems too, but for now, take Noah on your back to your nest for tonight, and maybe tomorrow we can meet back here and figure out a permanent home for him."

Noah was very proud to hear this, as it meant that he had made friends and, what's more, he had long decided to stay for some time, as he was learning so much and each day brought new ideas and adventures, even if some of them were frightening and tragic as the elephant episode had been. Staying here in his own home would be an advantage and he would not have to depend on the whims and kindness of others.

"Can you get onto my back and cling tightly?" asked the hoopoe.

"I can and it won't be the first time I have hitched a ride on some animal or bird's back," laughed Noah, as he expertly crawled onto the bird's smooth, feathered back and placed both paws around the crest of feathers that grew there.

Away the bird flew as Noah waved goodbye to Bengo, who proceeded to continue his search for ants and grubs in the turned over earth. Noah had a wonderful view of the plain far below and he could see, stretching off into the far distance, the rolling flat land disturbed only now and then by rocky outcrops just like the one that his friend Raina lived in. Raina! Events had happened so fast that Noah had forgotten all about his first friend that he had made since arriving here. He leaned in closely to Duma's ear and shouted over the wind, "Can you take me, please, to Raina the cheetah's home? I don't know exactly where it is, but if you can find it, I would be very grateful."

The bird called back, "As a matter of fact, I do know where she lives, it's over that way." And with that, Duma veered to the left and changed direction, flying into the setting sun.

"There it is, over there!" called the bird, but as they began to descend toward the rocky outcrop that Noah now recognized, it became apparent that something was terribly wrong.

Chapter 7

Cub Napped

THE DRIED GRASSES AROUND the carefully concealed cheetah den had been burned away, the opening to the lair was now pitifully exposed and the whole area was now bare, blackened and what was even more troubling, empty of any life at all.

"Please!" Noah shouted, "Let me down near the opening of the den."

The bird did so, landing not far from where Noah had spent his first night in that warm and cozy home. The hoopoe called out for Raina and took off to fly about the area to see, if any trace of the cheetah family could be found. Meanwhile, Noah scurried into the den calling out Raina's name.

When he got inside he could see that a great turmoil had taken place. The fur lined nest, in which Raina's babies had been curled up, was ripped apart with fur scattered all over the floor. Marks of a scuffle were visible on the entrance way and nest material was scattered all over the outside of the lair. What worried Noah most was the trail of blood that left the lair and continued on down the side of the hill and off into the grasses that grew beneath the rocky outcrop that had not been burned. The air reeked of the sharp smell of scorched grass and the wind blew black ash into Noah's face, as he frantically ran about calling for Raina.

Duma, at this point, flew back and landed beside Noah who, almost in tears, said, "We must find them. Can you keep flying about to see if you can spot any trace of them?"

"I cannot," said the bird in a kindly way, "I have to return to my nest and help my wife. She has been sitting on our eggs for many hours and now she has to have a break, as it is, I've been away too long. I'm sorry; I'll come back when I can."

The bird flew off leaving a distraught and frightened Noah, who now had to deal with the disappearance of a whole cheetah family. He sat down on the scorched earth, where he and Raina had spent time talking several evenings ago. Since then, Noah had met several other inhabitants of the savannah and witnessed their troubles and now, he was in the midst of turmoil, yet again. Poor Noah, kind, gentle and concerned animal that he was, he just could not see a way for him to help these animals and their problems for survival.

Sitting for a long period of time, Noah thought and thought but, for once could come up with nothing. His powers of imagination, his ability to read and understand human language did not seem to be of any use in this situation. Darkness fell and above, thousands of bright, sparkling stars came out and so clear and calm was the sky that Noah, in wonderment, felt that he could almost reach out and touch one of them. A soft warm breeze stirred the burnt tendrils of grass and again, as before, Noah felt that he was being spoken to. A whisper or a breath of air passing his tiny ears told him that he must persevere, he must not give up in despair and that he alone could bring help.

Noah sobbed tears of frustration, "But how can I? What do you want of me; I'm just one tiny mouse!" His faint voice was lost in a gust of sudden wind that again blew black ash around and reminded

Noah that he must keep looking for Raina and her family. Tired and disheartened, Noah curled up into as tiny a ball as he could and fell asleep right there, alone and exposed under the starry night sky. Exposed he was to all sorts of danger, but something was protecting him from all harm and, although he didn't understand it, a greater power of nature was watching over him.

Awakening with a start to the sounds of birds welcoming the sunny morning, Noah realized what a foolish thing he had done in leaving himself open to any predator that might come along. He had been so exhausted that he had fallen asleep without taking any precautions. Noah felt refreshed by his sleep and, after grooming himself and, getting rid of the black ash that had soiled his fur, he found some unburned seeds and filled himself with them. That, and a lick or two of early morning dew from under some rocks and he felt fit and ready for the day ahead.

The first thing that he felt he should do was to find a home for himself and, after examining the cheetah's empty lair, he decided that, even though it was very large for a small mouse, it would be an ideal home. He gathered some of the fur lining that had been scattered about and hauling it inside, he built a warm cozy nest for himself at the very back of the lair just under and behind the rock shelf that protruded from the wall. Here he could store seeds and keep himself warm, dry and protected from any eyes that might decide to explore the now empty den. Noah knew that the burnt grass would quickly grow back and add further protection and eventually would become a source of food.

After all his labours, Noah sat on top of the rocky outcrop surveying the grassy plain as far as the eye could see. He watched as herds of wildebeest, springboks and elands grazed peacefully upon the vast plain stretching off into the hazy distance, and he could even make out a family of lions stretched out beneath a grove of trees, resting and shielded from the relentless hot sun. Noah was fascinated to see white birds, called egrets, land upon the backs of various animals and peck at their hides. The animals did not seem to mind this and even looked as though they enjoyed these piggyback riders. Then Noah realized that the relationship worked both ways, the birds were pecking insects that burrowed into the skin of the animals and so, while this was a source of food for them, it also relieved the animal of a painful and unwanted guest.

Noah watched all of this and as he did so, he also realized that there was a plan working here: that each animal had its place and all were part of one great working organism . . . every being here depended upon the existence of another, whether it was a predator or prey and, if even one of the animal species was wiped out, the rest would feel the effects. If all the cheetahs and lions were to be wiped out, then the grazing antelopes that provided them with their food would multiply and then overgraze the grassland which, in turn, would leave the land underneath unprotected and it, in turn, would dry out and be lost to the wind or carried away by the annual rains. Finally the entire area could become a dried out desert with no animals or vegetation at all.

Noah thought all of this through and, as he sat and watched life unfold itself, a tremendous sense of the wonder of the natural life overcame him. He was lost in this thought, when a movement above him caught his attention and he immediately was on his guard. If Madame Topol had taught him anything, it was that he must always be on the lookout for what might come from above, be it hawks or owls or eagles, any one of which would love a tender mouse snack.

Noah understood about predators and prey, but he had no intention of being part of nature's way just yet. He ducked under the protective overhang of his new den and watched carefully to see what might descend from the sky. He was very relieved to see that it was Duma who landed nearby and called a cheery note of hello.

"I've just come from my nest. Let me tell you, did I catch it yesterday from my wife! She almost left me, she was so angry at my being late."

"I hope all is well now," answered Noah.

"Oh yes, I promised her a special gift of termites tonight. She is a pushover for termites, it wins her every time. But I have really come to tell you that I think that I have spotted what looks like it could be Raina."

"Oh, wonderful, where is she? Are the little ones with her? Is it far?"

The questions tumbled out of Noah so fast that Duma stopped him and said, "I don't know the answers to all of that, you had better hop on and see for yourself."

So, once again, Noah climbed up onto the back of a willing transport, and soon they were sailing high above the plain.

"Down there, look down there," called Duma to Noah over the rush of air sent by her beating wings.

Noah peered down at the grassy plain rushing past below, but could see nothing but dried grasses and several hyenas circling a clump of shrubs.

"There, where the hyenas are! That's where I thought I saw Raina this morning. I'm going to land so we can get a better look, but be very careful of those hyenas, they are fearless and vicious."

The bird landed not far from the circling animals and tried to appear disinterested as he, with Noah so small as to be nearly invisible, huddled against his back feathers, hopped as closely to them as he could.

"Clear off bird! We were here first, and we aren't in a sharing mood today," shouted one of the spotted brown and black animals with a shrill voice that sounded to Noah as a half laugh, half cough.

"Yes, fly away home, little bird! There is nothing here for you, we saw this cheetah first and when she breathes her last, we'll move in for the feast."

"It's going to be a good one," spoke up the third dog-like animal. Licking his lips and sneering at the hoopoe that now had edged closer to the dense screen of leaves that were hiding something within. "I'm going to ask all my relatives to this banquet, I wonder how much longer it'll be, before she gives up and we can safely go in and start feeding. I haven't had a square meal since last week when we found that dead antelope."

"I'm going in now, my mouth is watering for fresh meat, I'm so tired of rotted corpses that we are expected to clean up," this came from the fourth hyena who had just run up to join the pack.

"You will wait your turn like everyone else or get none at all," said the first hyena, who seemed to be the leader. "I'm the one who found this dinner and I'll be the one who has first choice, so stand aside, while I check to see if she is still breathing," with that, he began to sidle, with a nasty look at Duma, into the screen of leaves.

Noah, without a moment's hesitation, jumped off the hoopoe's back and stood as tall as he could upon his hind legs and shouted out with all his might, "Stop right where you are! Don't make one more move, in the name of Gaia!"

As though suddenly paralysed, the pack of animals all stopped, frozen to the spot. There was a long silence as they peered around to find out from whence came this unexpected voice mentioning the name of Gaia. Finally, the leader spotted the tiny mouse standing in amidst the clumps of grass.

"And just who might you be, morsel of food mouse?" Who are you to mention the name of Gaia in our midst? Speak up and quickly, we are hungry and can't wait for an insignificance like yourself to stop us from feeding."

"Gaia has sent me and I am here to put a stop to you. Now stand aside, while I enter this clump of bushes to find my friend Raina."

The hyenas were quite dumbfounded at this sudden turn of events and even more surprised at the mention of Gaia which filled them with awe and wonder.

"Gaia has sent you, a mere mouse to stop us, the clean-up crew of the savannah," sputtered the first hyena, whose name, by the way, was Hamir.

The other grunted in agreement and darted hostile glances at Noah, but did not move as though they were rooted to the spot.

"Yes, Gaia has sent me, and now, I'll thank you kindly to move aside to let me and my friend, Duma, go in to see what we can do for Raina."

The hyenas very grudgingly moved aside with many muttered curses and evil looks, as Noah and Duma scampered and hopped into the clump of shrubs and were soon lost to view. "Well, I never thought I would see the day when a mere mouse could come here and stop us from completing the work that Gaia herself has bidden us to do, act as clean up for the whole savannah."

"I agree, how can we be expected to do our job if we are sent interferences like this presumptuous little rodent who, ordinarily I would either ignore completely or chase for a quick pick-me-up lunch?"

"Well, I, for one, must think about getting back to my young, perhaps I can find some carrion along the way or else they are going to go without a meal tonight," said another, very dejected hyena. "You know, I really do not understand it, everyone hates and shuns us whenever we appear to do our work, but can you imagine the state of this place if we didn't clean up and get rid of all leftover kills and fallen animals?"

"Right you are, the plains would be a filthy and unliveable place but that's the way it is, animals like us are never appreciated. Well, let's go and see what else there might be for us, the day is young and there may be other kills to feast on once the lions or the leopards are through with them.

The pack moved off and trotted across the flatland, their snouts lifted to the wind to catch the scent of a rotted carcass, their eyes ever alert for a freshly killed animal that had been abandoned by its predator and left for the scavengers.

"Meanwhile, Noah and Duma searched the area hidden by the thick screen of vegetation. Noah kept calling, "Raina, Raina where are you? Are you hurt? Are you here?"

Finally, a faint moan could be heard coming from beneath a low hanging tree, whose branches swept the ground and provided a very private place for an animal to hide. Here, Noah found Raina, and what he saw shocked and saddened him. Raina lay, stretched out under the shade and protection of the tree, her long tongue hung out at an odd angle and she panted with great effort. Noah could see her side, where a rifle shot had torn open her hide, leaving a gaping wound that oozed a trickle of blood. Dried blood had coated the grass around where she lay. Raina spoke with effort, her once bright and alert eyes dimmed and dull with pain, "Oh Noah, the worst possible thing has happened. When I returned to my lair the other evening after leaving you with the elephants, I found the outcrop surrounded by men, poachers who had nets, rifles, and were surrounding my home. I leapt past them and into my lair to protect my little ones and," . . . and here she paused for breath.

"Take your time, there is no rush," said Duma.

"Oh yes, there is, you don't know everything that has happened, my babies, my poor, poor babies, whatever has become of them?" And here Raina broke off sobbing uncontrollably.

Noah stood by her helplessly stroking the matted and dirt encrusted fur of the cheetah's shoulder. "We are here, we can help," he soothed, but inwardly he felt that there was little that he could do. "Please try to tell us everything and we'll see what can be done."

"Water, if I could only have some water," panted the wounded animal.

Noah looked helplessly at Duma who said, "I can't bring you water, but I can bring you a juicy fruit from a tree not far from here that I know of, I'll fly there and bring one back in my beak as fast as I can." He flew off without another word leaving Noah to hear the rest of the story.

The cheetah gathered all her strength and half rose into a sitting position and continued with great effort, "I leapt into the lair and stood guard over my babies, but then I smelled smoke and I went out to investigate and found that the men had built a fire around the entrance. When I appeared, one of the men aimed a rifle at me and shot me. I fell over on my side and found that I couldn't move, the pain and the loss of blood was so great. While I lay there in agony, the rest of the men stamped out the fire, entered the lair and I had to watch in helpless pain, as they roughly snatched my innocent babies, who were so young they had never even been out into the sun. They called out for me and I lay there thrashing about and snarling, but my back legs seemed paralysed and I could barely move. The men just laughed and slung the babies who were crying piteously, into a dirty sack, ran off down the hill and that's the last I saw of them."

"I lay there for the longest time, trying to lick the wound and finally, when night came, I managed to crawl off and I found this hiding place where I've been ever since, trying to regain my strength and to think about what I can do." The cheetah collapsed now and lay still with exhaustion.

Before Noah could react to this tragic tale, Duma arrived with a large fruit clamped in his mouth. "Here you are, try eating this, it's juicy and will help take away your thirst."

He dropped the fruit in front of the prone animal who gratefully snapped it up and crushed it between jaws that were more used to crushing bones, hide and flesh. With purple juice trickling from her mouth, the cheetah thanked the kindly bird.

"I can bring you more fruit later," he said, "Just tell me when you need it."

"Thank you so much. I will repay your kindness someday if ever I am able to regain my strength, but how will I do that, I do not know. I'll need food and I can't hunt, while I am laid up like this."

The once proud and mighty cheetah now subsided into uncontrollable sobs, tears for her lost family and tears for her absolute helplessness. Noah, ever the practical thinker, said, "Could you manage to eat only fruit, if Duma could bring you some everyday?"

The cheetah looked up with scorn in her tear-filled eyes, "Fruit, you say fruit! I, a mighty hunter of meat, should eat fruit?"

Noah considered the animal's pride and said gently, "Well, I'm too small to hunt as is Duma, so really for now, fruit might be the best and only thing we can do until you regain your strength, and then we can figure out some way to return your family to you."

This last somewhat changed the fallen cheetah's attitude and she realized that her condition allowed no place for pride. "Well, I guess it wouldn't be so bad at that, I'll just have to get used to it. Thank you so much, you are true friends."

At that point, Noah, who had thought things through, came up with a plan. "Could you possibly get together enough strength to get back up the rise to your old lair?" he asked. "Because if you could, you could get better there in comfort, I can watch over you and warn against any enemies and Duma here can fly in with regular supplies of food. What do you think?"

"I think that is the best and only idea. Let us wait until nightfall so no one will see me. I'll rest for the remainder of the day and then we can move when the sun goes down."

And so the rest of the day was spent with Duma flying in with fresh fruit as often as he could take time from his own duties as a father waiting on his four eggs being tended by his wife. Noah passed the time back at the lair, trying in his small way to rearrange it and make it as comfortable as he could for the returning large animal. With his tiny mouth he laboriously brought in dried grasses and any other nest making material he could find, assisted by the hoopoe, who generously donated soft feathers from his own breast, to line the hollow that had until recently held the young family. When he finally felt that it was as comfortable as he could make it, he called for Duma, and after climbing on his back, they went for Raina. The three waited until nightfall and, with the bird flying ahead to scout for danger and Noah riding on Raina's back, they made their laborious way through the scrub of the savannah and, at last, up the hill to the lair. They had to stop very often, as the great cat was still very weak and needed to rest to gather her strength as often as she could.

The cheetah was very appreciative of Noah's efforts and she sank into the soft downy bed made for her with a sigh of gratitude, but being back in her home without her kittens brought on a fresh flood of tears.

"Where, oh where are my babies?" she moaned between sobs, "I'm so helpless here, if only I knew where they were. They are so young and innocent, not even out of their nest as yet. What will I do, when will I be able to go to them?"

All this sent daggers through Noah's kindly little heart. He felt such sorrow for the distraught cat but could think of nothing to do. "We will sit out front while you get some rest," he said to Raina, and the hoopoe and the mouse went out to leave the cheetah to cry herself to sleep.

Chapter 8

Noah Learns About Poachers

A S THE TWO SAT on the little hill overlooking the plain, Noah asked questions that had been bothering him for a while, but because he had been so busy, he hadn't had time to sit down and ask about. Now the setting sun painted a vivid picture of violent reds, greens, yellows and purples, as it filtered through the layers of clouds and cast a soft light over the land. They watched as a herd of elephants marched single file on their way to the river for water and Noah wondered, if this was the same herd that he had met and he thought about the terrible events of the other night and the awful sadness of the mother elephant that had lost her only child.

As a flock of birds winged their silent way across the slowly darkening sky, Noah turned to Duma and said, "Please tell me about poachers. What are they and why do they snatch the young of animals like Raina?"

"You mean you don't know what poachers are all about? You have led a sheltered life on your farm far away . . . did you not have poachers there?"

"No, I don't think so, at least I had never heard of anyone called a poacher."

"Well, poachers are the most dangerous and deadly enemies that we have," chirped Duma. "Mind you, as I have said, they really don't bother me very much, as I can fly and my nest is high in a tree and hard to get at. Anyway, there is no market for hoopoe babies."

"Please explain about everything: poachers, markets and all," said Noah, although he felt that he had a good idea about what was really going on.

"Well, poachers are hired by zoos far away to capture baby animals and take them away to live in cages for humans to come look at."

"How awful," said Noah, shuddering at the idea of spending a life in a cage.

"That's not all they do, it gets worse," continued the bird, "Sometimes the poachers don't even bother to take the babies. Sometimes they will kill the mother elephant or the mother rhino just for their tusks or horns, and then they leave the young to starve to death. Can you imagine the trouble if one of us were to steal off with one of the humans' children? If that happened then they would punish all of us with poison, fire and traps." the bird continued. "We are completely helpless here on the plain, there is no protection for us and nowhere for us to go. Sometimes wealthy humans from across the sea come here just to shoot the larger animals for no reason other than to put their heads on display in their homes. What a disgusting idea!"

The bird fell silent and the two stared out at the now dark scene, thinking their own thoughts about the ways of life and the problems that existed here in this primitive and natural place.

Duma started up, fluttered his wings and said, "I must be off, it's near my turn on the eggs. I'll be so glad when they are hatched; just sitting on eggs can be so boring".

The two said goodbye with Duma promising to drop by with some more fruit in the morning. They both knew that the cheetah would eventually regain her strength, but it would be a long time, as she had no access to fresh meat which would have restored her to health much faster than fruit as it is not a cheetah's regular diet. Noah continued to sit, enjoying the cool evening breeze that blew; it was such a relief after the hot dry wind of the day. An idea was brewing in his mind and, after saying good night to a bird who nested nearby, he entered the lair and curled up in his tiny nest where he slept soundly until the early morning, when he was awakened by the usual noise of the flocks of tiny and brightly colored finches that roosted in a grove of trees not far away. Noah opened his eyes and the first thing he could see was the cheetah curled up in the open entrance to the lair. The cat saw Noah and tried to smile, but the smile turned into a sad and bitter look.

"Good morning, Noah. Did you spend a good night?" she asked and before Noah could reply, she continued, "I slept a good sleep and I must say that I feel so much better, I'm ready to plan a way to find my babies."

Noah smiled and said, "I'm glad to hear it. Would you like some fruit? Duma has left some just outside the lair."

Raina pulled a face and said, "I hate fruit, I'd love some raw antelope, but I guess beggars can't be choosers." And she made her painful way out of the lair and into the bright sunshine of the new day.

Noah followed after her and, when he was sure that Raina had filled herself with fruit, he sat down beside her. He had learned that it isn't wise to talk to or bother animals, while they are eating. They are nervous and apt to snarl and snap until they have had their fill and are relaxed. "Raina," he began, "I've been thinking, and I might have a plan about your babies."

Before he could go on, Raina interrupted with a glad growl of joy. "Oh, Noah, I knew that you would come up with something, you are such a dear friend, and I thank Gaia that you were sent to me."

Noah tried to stop this outpouring of optimism because, while he did have a small plan, he certainly could not guarantee that he would, in any way, be able to either find the missing babies or, even if he did, could return them to their mother. He now tried to calm the excited cheetah.

"Raina, please don't believe that this is going to be the end of your troubles. There is no guarantee that I'll be able to find your babies, but I will try. If Duma will fly me, we can survey the whole area from above and perhaps, just perhaps, we will see something that can help us."

Noah did not want to get Raina's hopes too high, as he really did not know what else he could do beyond trying to see where the poachers were camped, and if they still had the little ones with them. Duma flew in at this point and landed with a small flutter beside them, his beak stuffed with the fruit that Raina needed but didn't much like.

"Thank you, but I will be so glad, when I can hunt myself and return to eating good raw meat," she purred in as grateful a sound as she could manage.

Noah now began to outline his plan to Duma who said, "Well, it sounds fine to me, but you have to understand that I can't be gone for too long a time. My wife told me this morning that she could hear tiny sounds from our eggs and that it won't be too long, until they are getting ready to hatch, and then my time will be spent finding food for them and I won't be able to be with you as often or as much."

"We quite understand," said Noah, "so maybe we had better get started right away."

"Let's be off then," cried Duma and without any further chat, Noah was on his back where he now felt as comfortable, as if he had always ridden there.

"Good bye and good luck!" waved Raina, who for the first time since being wounded looked a little like her old self.

The two were soon aloft and were flying low over the vast plain that made up this part of East Africa.

CHAPTER 9

In the Enemy Camp

NOAH THRILLED AS HE saw the huge herds of animals that grazed upon the dried grasses, and he could see lions, warthogs, packs of wild dogs and other familiar animals going about their daily business. As they flew on toward the river, they passed over a herd of elephants on their way to drink. Noah again wondered if this was the same herd that he had met the other night, and if the mother who had lost her baby was with them. He had little time to wonder for, just ahead of them, rose up the strangest animal that Noah had yet seen. It had long, long legs and a neck that seemed to stretch upward forever, ending in a small head with large brown eyes and small ears. The animal's body was spotted with dark brown patches against a white background. As Duma approached the animal, he fluttered about its head.

"Good morning, Gamal," said the bird, "Please meet my friend, Noah. We're on our way to find some poachers. Have you seen anybody suspicious about in the last while?"

Gamal glanced at Noah clinging to the bird's back and smilingly said, "Hello, pleased to make your acquaintance. Are you from around here?"

The bird was now hovering at eye level with the tallest animal Noah had ever seen, and he was pleased that this new friend did not seem in the slightest surprised to find a mouse riding on a bird's back.

"No, I am from far away and I'm pleased to meet you."

Duma said, "He has been sent by Gaia to come here."

"Welcome, if Gaia sent you, you must be a special animal, and yes, I have seen something suspicious going on down by the watering hole by the river. There were several men there yesterday and I could see, although I did not like to get too close, that they were not the usual fishermen but that they had nets, and I could see rifles. I think that they might have a camp near there. I hope that has been of some help to you."

"Yes it has, and thanks so much," chirped out the bird and, with a flutter of his wings in goodbye, he flew off again in the direction of the river.

Noah could now see before him the line of bright green that indicated moisture and abundant growth following the river's path. It was now the dry season and, although the river had shrunk to one quarter its usual size, there was still enough water to satisfy the needs of the animals from the plain. They now flew directly over the river and Noah could see crocodiles sunning themselves along the muddy banks and he shuddered inside, as he knew from his readings about African wildlife, that these animals were very vicious and wondered if any mention of Gaia would stop them from making a meal of him, if the opportunity arose. He hung onto Duma's back a little more tightly now, as they flew lower down and along the bank of the meandering river.

Different animals could be seen here, drinking or frolicking about. Nearby, a noisy troop of baboons squealed, jeered and called out swear words at the low flying bird. "Ignore them," said Duma, "they are so ignorant and just love to make a lot of noise and trouble. I dread them anywhere near my nest."

49

Further along, a family of hippopotamus were rolling about and having a wonderful time in the shallow edges of the water. They snorted and opened their huge mouths with their gapped large teeth, and then would submerge and, after what would seem like a very long time, they would surface with a lot of splashing with their mouths full of water plants."

"They look harmless and like great fat babies, but they are very dangerous, perhaps not to you and I, but humans have to be very careful around them," said Duma, as they flew past the wallowing hippos and on down the river.

Ahead, a thin stream of smoke could be seen coming from deep within a clump of very dense trees . . . They flew over this and down in amongst the forest vegetation they darted. Ahead and below them, they could make out a camp. A fire smouldered over which several pots were hung and, off to one side, were several tents strung up under the protection of the leafy trees. Behind the tents were many cages made of bamboo, a very soft and easily bent wood. The cages appeared to be covered with branches and grass, perhaps to hide them from prying eyes. No humans could be seen and Noah was rather glad about that, as it meant that they could get down for a better look with out having to worry about having to hide from anyone.

They landed near the tents and Duma said, "You check out those cages, while I see what is in these tents."

Noah quickly agreed and set off in the direction of the cages which were nearer to the river. He kept close to the trees and shrubs bordering the clearing, as he was not entirely sure that the poachers were absent. As he cautiously moved closer, he could hear what sounded like whimpering over the sounds of the busy river with its bird song and the constant chatter of monkey families in the trees.

When he got to the cages, he climbed up to the top where there was a wire screen over the cage itself to allow in air and light. When he looked below through the gloom, he could dimly make out the two missing cheetah cubs. They were huddled together in one corner of the cage, and it was their whimpering that Noah had heard earlier.

Noah called gently down to them, "Hi, remember me? I'm your mother's friend and I've come to try to help you."

The cheetah babies looked up at Noah and when they recognized him, they did not hiss and draw back as they had done in their lair.

They leapt up and stretched as high as they could with their paws against the side of the cage, so that their faces were inches from Noah's.

"We are so glad to see you, we don't understand what is being done to us," said one.

"Those men do not feed us what we are used to and this cage is cold and uncomfortable. We want our mother," wailed the other, and they both collapsed to the bottom of the grass lined cage in a heap of sobs and whimpers.

Noah felt so sorry for them that he rashly promised, "Don't worry; I'll do my best to get you back to your mother."

At this very moment, a hand that seemed to come out of nowhere reached down and grabbed hold of Noah. None too gently, the hand picked him up and held him close to a very ugly scarred face covered with coarse whiskers. Noah's first reaction was to tell the man in human language to put him down, but then common sense told him that he should keep this ability quiet, until he might need it later on. He was held there upside down while the man examined him. Noah could smell alcohol on his breath as he finally spoke.

"Well. Well. Well. What have we here? A little mouse who wants into the cheetah cage! Well, you will make a nice lunch for them and save me the trouble of having to catch one. The cage had a latch on the side that Noah had not noticed and, without any further ceremony, the man flipped open the latch, opened the cage door a crack and tossed Noah in. He landed on top of the two huddled little cheetahs and he quickly scampered off them and over to the far side of the narrow cage. As he was not entirely sure what their reaction would be.

He was reassured, however, when one of them said, "Don't worry, we aren't going to harm you. You are our mother's friend and are here to help us."

With his mind at ease, Noah had the presence of mind to crawl beneath the grass matting that covered the floor, that way the human would think that he had been instantly devoured. Sure enough, the human peered in and, seeing no mouse, said, "A nice lunch for my two fine, young, money makers. Now you two, look sharp, as the buyer is coming this afternoon and I want to get top dollar for you."

Another rough looking man approached the cages and, with a sneering voice said, "How much money do you think we're going to make with this haul of animals? Let's see, we have the two cheetahs, four baby crocodiles, a little baboon, eight grown monkeys and a fully grown crocodile, along with about ten or twelve snakes of different kinds. Not bad for a week's work."

"Should be enough to have ourselves a little holiday on the beach, before coming back for the next load," said the first man. "This area is a good one, because, not only are there a lot of animals to help ourselves to, there aren't any pesky police to stop and arrest us."

"Yeah," replied the other, "that's the best. We can raid nests, rob babies and snare older animals. It's a good thing too. The last time I spent in jail, I vowed it would be the last. What time is that agent supposed to be here?"

"Anytime soon, let's have our lunch and then get these boxes out into the sun, so that he can have a good look at our wild little friends here." The two moved off toward the tents, laughing to themselves about how easy it was to make a good living poaching dumb animals.

Noah, still crouched underneath the grass matting, had heard all this and, because he understood human language, knew what they were talking about and he knew that if he were to act, it would have to be soon, or the animals would be gone. Duma flew up at this point calling for Noah, who replied that he was locked up inside the baby cheetah cage.

"How ever did you get in there?" Before Noah could rely, he said, "I was inside their tent, what a disgusting mess, if I kept a nest as foul as that, I would never have attracted the mate that I have."

"There isn't any time for chat," shouted Noah, "can you use your beak to unhitch the catch on the side of the cage?"

Duma hopped to the side of the cage and tried to lift the hook with his beak, but it seemed too heavy.

Please hurry," called Noah, "they may return at any time."

By this time, the animals in the nearby cages had heard the conversation between Noah and Duma and they became increasingly excited at the thought that they may be set free. They began to call out in their various voices for help, "Don't forget about us. Let us out. Please free me also," came the cries and Noah was very afraid that this outbreak of noise would bring the poachers running.

Sure enough, one of the men came back and shouted angrily, "Shut up all of you, make any more noise and I'll give you something to shout about." He gave the nearest cage a vicious kick and it fell over onto its side.

This cage happened to be the one that contained the cheetahs and Noah. The hoopoe fluttered back from the bushes, where he had been hiding and tried the latch again. This time he was able to flip it out of the hook. The kick had loosened it enough to make it easy to open. Noah now took charge, as he realized that the two cheetah babies were too young to be of any help and he saw that they were willing to do whatever he told them.

"Quickly, push hard against the wire mesh of the cage door, so that it will open wide enough to let you squeeze out."

One of the young cheetahs did so and soon found himself half in and half out of the cage. "Push harder," said Noah and the door fell open and the cheetah tumbled out into the clearing. Soon Noah and the remaining cheetah joined him and there was precious time wasted while the two babies tumbled about, joyful at their freedom.

Noah realized that he was going to have to take the role of parent in this situation, as the little ones could not seem to take any responsibility for themselves. With a stern voice, Noah ordered the two to stop their fooling and to get into the shrubs as fast as they could, so that they would be out of sight should the men come back again. The two did as they were told, hiding themselves as best they could.

"What now?" asked Duma, "How are you, a tiny mouse going to transport two helpless cubs back to their mother?"

"I'll tell you in a moment, but first, help me free all of these other animals. I can't go off and leave them."

The other animals had become very quiet after the harsh visit of their captor, although they did not understand what he said. They could tell from the tone of his voice that he had promised punishment and so they, very sensibly, lay low in their cages and waited for whatever was going to happen. They could understand Noah, because he spoke nature natter and they knew that help might be at hand. Although they could hear him, they could not see him and so had no idea that a mouse might save them. At this point, Duma became very angry.

"I'll not be part of saving baboons and monkeys," he said, thrusting out his beak aggressively, "I've been a good sport and done all I could for Raina, but I will not help animals who would raid my nest and eat my eggs or babies."

Noah thought quickly, "But you must keep helping, please. After all, Gaia is counting on you!"

This somewhat softened Duma's cold attitude and so he grudgingly said, "Well, I will open the cages and I'll help you return the babies to Raina but then, that's it, no more. I will not lift a claw for a monkey or a snake, they are on their own."

Noah thought that this was the best that he could hope for right now and so he said, "Right, just flip open the cage doors and we will leave them to escape on their own."

The bird then went from cage to cage opening the latches of all of them. Some were easy, others harder and took more effort, some Noah had to help, using all the strength he could muster in his tiny paws. After what seemed a very long time and after a great deal of effort, all of the cage doors were opened and, with Noah on his back, Duma flew onto a protective low hanging branch and called out to the various animals, who had crawled, hopped or slithered out of their respective cages and were now all about the clearing in a daze, not quite sure where to go or what to do with this newfound and unexpected freedom.

"All of you pay very careful attention," called out Duma, as loudly as he could. "You have all been set free thanks to my friend here, Noah, who has been sent by Gaia to help us animals. You must thank him and give him safe passage, whenever you see him. If it were not for him, you would all be sold by those wicked men to zoos and kept in cages far from your homes for the rest of your lives."

The various animals looked up to see Noah who was perched on Duma's back. They called out their thanks in their various voices, except for the crocodile whose heart even the mention of Gaia could not soften or move. She lumbered off and slid down the bank of the river to disappear beneath the water, calling the four young crocodiles to follow her.

The other animals began to disperse to their various homes. The snakes soon slithered out of sight into the underbrush. The monkeys and baboons called their goodbyes and thanks and were soon swinging from branch to branch away from the site of their imprisonment as fast as they could.

"I'm sorry but I have to go too, my eggs are hatching and I have to be there to help." said Duma. "But you had better get out of here as fast as you can. The poachers will be back soon and you do not want to be caught here, when they find all of their captured loot gone." He fluttered up to a tree branch and waved his wing in farewell, "Take good care, I'll come visit you at Raina's lair. Goodbye."

Like an arrow, he was off and out of sight, leaving one rather confused Noah searching the bushes for the two hidden cheetah cubs.

"Come out wherever you are," he whispered in as loud a voice as he dared and, after several moments, out came the two very frightened cubs.

"Will you look after us, please?" cried one.

"Will you feed us and take us back to our mother, please?" whimpered the other.

Noah knew that no matter what might befall him, he would do his very best to save them from the poachers and return them to their mother. He decided that they must set off immediately, and so he arranged to seat himself on the shoulder of one of the cubs and to try to find their way through the grassy savannah to Raina's lair. He really did not know which way to go first as, having flown in, he had not noticed any landmarks except for one, the river, and he decided to follow it upstream as best he could. It would mean travelling through dense forest and over marshy, wet swamp, but once Noah made up his mind, then that was it. He would do his best.

CHAPTER 10

A Return Home

THEY QUICKLY LEFT THE clearing and disappeared into the trees surrounding it. It was a lucky thing that they left when they did as, sure enough, the poachers returned and, when they found that their captured animals had all disappeared, their rage was indescribable. They shouted, yelled and even blamed each other for carelessness, finally coming to blows and wrestling one another on the dusty ground. After a bloody nose and many bruises, the two lay exhausted, staring up at the tree top.

"What do we do now?" panted one.

"I guess we had better stop fighting and get into our truck and see what we can catch before the buying agent gets here. He is going to be furious when he finds out that he has come all this way from the city for nothing. Let's get going and see what we can find."

The two got up, dusted themselves off and headed for the old, beat up truck that they used to transport their stolen cargo in. The truck emerged from the clearing, just at the exact moment that Noah and the cubs were trying to cross the trail to get to the other side and into the forest. The truck rattled and bounced along until the poacher who was not driving shouted, "Look, look there! There are the two cheetah cubs, stop and let's try to catch them. They're young and can't get far in this heavy underbrush."

The truck came to a very sudden halt and the two men, armed with rifles and a net, jumped out and gave chase to the cubs.

Noah, seeing that they were sure to be caught, said, "Don't be afraid, I'll not ever leave you." He said this more to reassure himself than anything, as he knew that the men would shoot, if they couldn't catch them.

He urged the cubs to run but the two, being so young, really did not have any idea about hiding or the ways of avoiding capture. Very soon, the two, with Noah hidden in the fur of one, were netted and lay in a heap crying, whimpering and spitting at the triumphant poachers who were jubilant at having regained at least this much of their lost loot.

"These two should catch a great price on the open market," said one, as he tied the net securely imprisoning the cheetahs.

"They won't get away now," vowed the other, as he heaved the net with the struggling cubs into the back of the truck.

They landed with a very big bump and, having the breath knocked out of them, they lay quietly, the struggle all out of them. Noah appeared from the fur under which he had hidden.

"Don't fight. Don't give them any reason to hurt you, they are very angry at losing all the other animals and so will not be in a mood to be gentle if you annoy them." He had no idea as to what to expect next, but he knew that he must quieten the whimpering cubs and try to comfort them as best he could. The two men got back into the cab of the truck and soon it was on its way, jouncing over the rough terrain of the savannah,

During the time that the truck had stopped and the two men were chasing the cubs and finally netting them, a long line of elephants had emerged from the trees lining the river, where they had spent the morning bathing. They were on their way now to feed in a grove of trees not far away, which their leader, Vashti, knew about. When she saw the truck with its human occupants, she trumpeted angrily and the herd soon took up the cry. The terror of the other night when they had lost one of their children was still fresh in their minds and now, seeing humans, even if they were not the same men who had killed the baby elephant, enraged them and the trumpet called for revenge and attack.

Soon the herd of gigantic, grey beasts was thundering its way directly in line with the truck. When the driver saw that the herd was headed his way and obviously with terror on its mind, he put his foot on the gas and tried to outrun them. The trail was one used by buffaloes and was not meant for the machines of man and so it was rough and it was not at all straight. Soon the driver found himself off the trail and heading across the open plain.

With a terrible bang, the truck hit a large hole that had been dug recently by a badger who wanted to dig a burrow for himself. The truck was going so fast that, when it hit the hole, it soared into the air and fell onto its side, its wheels spinning and the radiator spouting steam and shooting hot water into the air.

The elephants did not stop but galloped up to the overturned truck and came to a halt beside it, all the while trumpeting and bellowing their anger. Now they milled around the fallen vehicle, their ears flapping majestically, their trunks raised in triumph. They began to butt and stomp on the truck with their huge trunk-like feet, kicking and shoving the small truck again and again in their anger at this intrusion by humans into their world. The net containing the cubs fell out of the open trunk of the truck and Vashti trumpeted for a stop to the attack.

"What is this" she bellowed. "Two tiny cheetahs captured by these cruel and heartless men? Wait while I untie the cords and set them free." She expertly untied the ropes with her sensitive trunk which could do the most delicate and intricate of operations. When the net fell open the two bruised and battered baby cheetahs tumbled out and lay in a frightened huddle as the herd gathered around and contemplated them.

Noah appeared from beneath the fur of one of the cubs and standing as tall as he could on the back of the cub said, "Thank you, in the name of Gaia, for saving us."

Vashti stepped forward saying, "I recognize you. You were with us the other night when we were attacked by those men with torches and guns."

"Yes, it was I, you had placed me on the fence post while you ate and we were to talk later."

"Well, our talk will have to wait again. What are you doing here with these two babies? Please don't tell me that you are working with these evil men."

"I certainly am not; I have been trying to return them to their mother, Raina, who was wounded by these same men."

"This is what is happening all over the savannah, our families are not safe and we are losing our rights to live and thrive as Gaia planned in our own home," moaned Vashti, as the elephants, with her, bellowed their agreement. "What can we do? Where can we go to be safe and secure?"

"The herd milled around pondering this, but came to a halt as one of the two men shoved and pushed his way out of the dented cab of the truck. They watched, as he pried open the other door and freed the second man who was badly hurt and lay on the ground moaning. Vashti stopped several of the younger elephants, who made as if to crush the men beneath their massive hoofs.

"No," she trumpeted, "While I would like to see them punished for the misery that they have inflicted upon us, it would be wiser to let them go free."

"Why should we allow them freedom," wailed the mother of the dead baby elephant, "Did they or their kind offer us any sympathy or understanding?"

"No, you are right, they did not, but they lack our wisdom and our understanding and furthermore, if we harm them, they and others will only come here and do further mischief upon us or other animals," said Vashti wisely. The other elephants grumbled amongst themselves, but they knew Vashti was their leader and finally subsided and obeyed her.

The first man out of the wreckage of the truck now helped the other to his feet and, with many a shaken fist and angry backward looks, they hobbled across the open plain. Now Vashti turned her attention to Noah and the two cubs.

"I know Raina and, although our lives take different paths, I know her to be a respectful animal that does her best to raise her family and live within the rules of Gaia. I will take you to her myself and, at least, we will know that one family is going to be happily reunited this day."

Vashti gave instructions to several of the elephants near her and they, their gigantic, ponderous bodies looking like huge grey mountains to tiny Noah, made their way with soft steps over to where the two cubs lay blinking in fear and wonderment. They cringed and did what they always did when frightened or unsure. They spat and hissed at the gigantic beasts looming over them.

"Don't be afraid" said Noah, who knew the thrill of being carried on an elephant's trunk, "They will not hurt you, and you'll find that it's fun riding up that high."

The cubs, who had come to trust Noah even through all the turmoil that they had undergone, now relaxed and allowed the elephants to lift them with wondrous gentleness and delicacy high up into the air. For the first time, Noah saw the two cubs meow with delight and enjoy an experience like no other. Vashti now took Noah up onto her back where he clung, grasping onto the coarse hairs that thinly cover all elephants. From here he could see the entire savannah and he felt just like an Indian Rahja, powerful and in control.

The herd set off in single file with Vashti leading and, after a long trek, passed herds of elands and various kinds of antelope all feeding peacefully. They came to the rocky outcrop that was the cheetah's home. They could see from far off that Raina was standing guard on the little hill, anxiously scanning the surrounding for any sight of Noah and her lost little ones.

When the line of elephants came nearer, she could see her offspring safely wrapped in the protective curl of the elephants' trunks and she almost forgot her pain and wounds in her delight and excitement at their return. The elephants gently set the two cubs down at the base of the hill and they, without a backward glance, raced headlong up to their mother who licked and purred her intense joy at having them back with her at last.

She tried to speak her thanks to the gigantic animals but was too choked up to say much but, "Thank you, thank you," over and over again.

Noah asked to be let down and as he stood in front of Vashti, she said to him, "Why don't you come with us and spend some time with me; we can talk and find out about each other's life."

Noah thought quickly about this and said, "I would really like that and I want to do it sometime but for now, I think it would be better for me to stay here close to Raina, just to help her if I can, and to get used to the tiny home I have made here as I really haven't had time to do so. Thank you so much for all that you have done and, perhaps in a week or so, when Raina has recovered from her wounds, I can come and visit you."

"Well you will be welcome, little mouse who thinks only of others. Goodbye and we will see you again soon."

The line of elephants slowly and carefully moved off and, after many waved and shouted goodbyes and thanks, they were soon lost to view, as the evening haze began to envelope the land. The cubs were so exhausted by the events of the day that soon after their mother fed them the nurturing milk that they had missed they fell into a deep and, for the first time, peaceful sleep.

Raina, who already had begun to look like her own fit self, sat with Noah at the lair's entrance, while he told her the whole story of the events of the day.

Raina purred her thanks and, when Noah fell asleep halfway through a sentence, she realized that he, too, had had a very tumultuous day; and so, as night descended, she picked him up gently in her mouth, as if he were one of her cubs, and with great and loving care, she laid him down in the tiny nest that he had built for himself further back in the cave. There, he slept a deep and restoring sleep until the usual chatter of the finch families awoke him at dawn the next morning.

CHAPTER 11

Monkey Business

F OR THE NEXT FEW days Noah did nothing but laze about the den
and spend time talking to Raina and to Duma, who had flown in
with more of the detested fruit that Raina needed to have but could
not stand to eat.

"I really feel that I am up to a hunt," she said.

"Not until you are completely healed," stated Noah, who felt a
trifle bossy when it came to the welfare of the cheetah family. "You
can't be racing about until that wound is completely healed over," he
said.

"Well, I don't know how much more fruit I can take. We cheetahs
are carnivores and that's what I need."

"What is a carnivore?" asked Duma.

"Someone who is a meat eater and eats meat only," replied Noah.

"Where do you come by all that knowledge that you have?" asked Raina. "You seem to know an awful lot for a mouse!"

Before Noah could answer, Duma spoke up: "No one has thought to ask me about my four beautiful chicks that were just hatched."

Noah felt badly about forgetting Duma's eggs in the excitement of bringing the cubs home. "I'm so sorry," he said. "How is your wife and did all go well?"

"Yes, all went well and now, I must be off to take my turn at bringing food to them. You can imagine how hungry they must be after spending all that time in an egg."

"Yes, I know how little ones can eat," said Raina fondly, as she watched her own two rolling about in a game of tag.

Duma flew up into a nearby bush saying, "I will be back tomorrow with more fruit for you. See you then!" and he flew off towards his home.

Raina rose and stretched. "I really think that I could hunt tomorrow, I must give it a try at least."

"Well, if you must go, at least take me with you," said Noah.

"You mean ride on my back, while I scout and attack an antelope? What if you fall off or get trampled? It can be very risky work you know."

"Yes, I know," replied Noah. "Don't forget the day we met, I was hitching a ride on you then, and I survived."

"Well, if you are sure, I don't want anything to happen to you, ever," said Raina looking at Noah as fondly as she regarded her own family. "You are one of us now and I do not want to lose you."

"Thanks," said Noah, he was very pleased that the fierce cheetah had taken such a liking to him. "I am very proud to be considered a member of your family."

The next morning, Raina rose as always with the first song of the birds and, as she stretched to loosen her muscles, she said to Noah, who was already awake and had been out in the early dawn to breakfast on seeds, "This is the day, I feel as I used to. My wound is healed over and I have rested well. I'm off to hunt." And with one final check on the two cubs and a stern warning that they were not to leave the lair under any circumstances, Raina, with Noah firmly settled on her back, strode confidently out of the lair and down from the rocky outcrop and out onto the plain. She slowly circled around a herd of antelope, but they were very wary today and stampeded off in a cloud of dust.

"It's so dry before the rains come," said Raina over her shoulder to Noah who was coughing and spitting out the dust that had got into his nose and mouth.

"The rains?" he asked, "When do they come? Is there a special time for rain?"

"Yes," replied the cheetah, gazing off into the distance to try to spot another source of prey. "The rains come every year at about this time and it rains for several weeks and then you will see everything turn green, flower and the whole plain comes alive."

Noah had noticed that the grass was dry and dead and that the river near the poacher's camp was nearly down to a trickle, and the elephants and the hippos were more often than not bathing in wet mud.

"Does the rain only come once a year?" he asked, thinking of home, where it would rain off and on year-round.

"Pretty much only once a year; we call it the rainy season or the monsoon and it isn't much fun when it's here but after, the whole world comes alive and makes it worthwhile."

As the cheetah prowled about the plain looking for prey, Noah noticed that they were getting closer and closer to the line of trees that followed the river bank. The leaves were dry and drooping in the great heat and no breeze seemed to come and stir the dry grass or to provide a cool relief from the oppressive warmth.

Noah had an idea. He felt that he was in the way of Raina and her hunt and that she was too polite to tell him, that, plus the discomfort he felt in the hot sun, which he was not used to, he said, "Why don't you take me to the river bank and I can look for Vashti and her herd? I promised that I would visit her and you can then get on with your hunt and pick me up later on your way back to the lair."

"Well, if you are sure you want to, I don't mind. Perhaps it might be better if you do that, then I can concentrate on my hunt more," replied Raina. And so she altered her direction and headed toward the bank of the river.

When she arrived at the shore, there were many warthogs, several tall giraffes and many, many birds of various kinds all having a drink of the brown syrup-like water.

The giraffe, Gamal, whom Noah had met before, strolled over and, bending his head very low to the level of Raina's, said, "Greetings Raina. It's good to see you back on your feet, after that terrible thing the poachers did to you and your family."

"Thank you, Gamal, but we really have to thank our hero here, Noah the mouse; he was the one who saved my babies."

Gamal smiled at Noah and fluttered his long, long lashes, "Hello, Noah, still here? You haven't gotten tired of us yet?"

Noah was embarrassed at the praise heaped on him by Raina and said, "Oh no, not tired of this wonderful and exciting place at all, but Raina is wrong. I'm not a hero, we have to thank Duma, the hoopoe, and Vashti, the elephant, for helping to find and save the cheetah cubs."

"So modest and so humble," said the giraffe, "well whatever, as long as the poachers are got rid of, that's all that really matters."

"Are they gone? Do you know?" asked Raina. "It would set our minds at ease to know."

"I think that their camp is still here deep in the woods but, even if they were gone, would it make any difference? Some more would only arrive to do the same killing and stealing." The tall spotted animal lifted up his head and began to stroll back to his mate. "I'll keep my eyes out for any sign of poachers and let you know," he said, as he made his graceful way back to his waiting mate. The two had one more drink before disappearing, their heads visible above the trees as they moved off.

Noah noticed the odd way that they used to drink: they had to position their two front legs very far apart in order for them to bend down low enough for each to touch the water with their mouths. 'They are lovely, gentle creatures,' thought Noah but did not say so as Raina, whom he loved dearly, needed to be a violent killer of innocent animals in order to live and, while this seemed hard for a mouse such as Noah to accept, he instinctively knew, that this was the way of nature and had to be accepted by all.

Raina had now drunk her fill and said, "This will be so much fresher after the rains send down more water. I must be off. Are you sure that you will be alright here waiting for Vashti and her herd?"

"I'll be fine, just please remember to come by and pick me up, when you have finished your hunt," said Noah.

"I'll be back as soon as I can, my friend." And she was off, her tail switching, her body low to the ground, her mind now totally concentrated on the stalk and the hunt before her.

Noah settled down on a fallen log, under which he saw that he could quickly run and hide if any danger approached. He was perfectly content to observe the various animals that arrived to drink. Among them were several impalas, an assortment of mongoose and several jackals and dog-like hyenas. There was a family of monkeys, who fought noisily and played boisterously in the trees above the water, every once in a while descending for a quick drink before racing off, chasing one another or swinging wildly from branch to branch. Noah watched enviously, thinking how much fun it would be to slide and glide so effortlessly from tree to tree, when a tiny member of that same family raced by, coming to a very sudden halt upon spotting Noah. It studied Noah quizzically for a few moments and then hopped over for a better look.

"Aren't you that brave little mouse that saved my brothers from the poachers' cages the other day?"

Before Noah could utter a sound, the tiny animal, with its long skinny tail, had raced up a nearby tree trunk and was whistling shrilly to the rest of the family. Soon Noah was surrounded by a whole pack of constantly moving monkeys who shoved, pushed and hopped on top of one another for a look.

"This is that mouse!" exclaimed the first one who had spotted Noah. "This is he who saved Simian and Nukky from the poachers. Come take a look."

From the mass of jostling and crowding monkeys, two pushed their way to the front to face a rather nervous Noah who wasn't at all sure of his safety.

"Yes, this is he, the one I told you all about," screeched out Nukky who indeed was one of the two that Noah had helped set free. "I told you all that it was a mouse and no one believed me. Well, here he is.

Hello, mouse, and thank you for saving me and my buddy, Simian, we are much indebted to you."

Noah realized that this jostling, ceaselessly jiggling about, hoard of monkeys wanted to do him no harm but were just curious and wanted to get a look at this marvel that they had heard about; a mouse who had saved several of their family from a terrible capture by poachers.

"Whoa, stop! Get back! Don't crowd!" shrilled Nukky, who placed a protective arm around Noah to fend off the inquisitive little monkey hands that reached out to touch this small and nervously shy mouse. "Come on, Noah, come with me and we'll go up into the treetops, so we can get away from this crowd. Be off! Be gone, you chattering fools."

He whistled and another monkey who, to Noah, looked just like all the rest, swung down from the branch on which he was seated and together they picked Noah up, without a by-your-leave and, before he knew what was happening, he found himself being carried high above the river to the tops of the tallest trees. "But, but," he protested, to no avail.

He was deposited on a branch from which he immediately slipped and fell. Plummeting faster than he could even think, he fell straight down past other monkeys, past leaves and branches and, just as he was about to hit the earth, a paw reached out and caught him by his tail. There he dangled; face downward until Nukky, who had raced down after him, scooped him up and raced back up the tree darting from branch to branch with one paw holding Noah high in the air, the other paw grabbing onto branches as his body and hind legs caught up. At last, a frightened and breathless Noah was again deposited on a topmost branch, but placed more securely than last time. While Noah was trying to both get his breath and restore his dignity, Nukky and Simian just chattered on as if nothing had happened.

"Well, here we are. We've got you all to ourselves and we can laugh and play up here all day long. Won't that be fun?"

Noah's head turned from one monkey to the other, as one would continue a sentence before the other had even finished, so rapidly did they speak.

"Please, wait a minute while I catch my breath," he protested.

"See, it's all your fault, carrying him up here so quickly."

"My fault! What about you? You let him drop and, if it hadn't been for me and my quick thinking, he would have hit the ground and then, where would we be?"

The two started to argue furiously and Noah thought they would have come to blows, so loudly did they shrill and, what with them moving about so much and the tree tops swaying back and forth, he felt himself slipping downwards again. When the two arguing monkeys saw Noah begin to fall they immediately stopped their quarrelling and two paws shot out to grab him and redeposit him on a broad, firm branch.

"Let's stop our silly argument and concentrate on Noah before we lose him again," said Nukky. Simian agreed and they both remained silent, looking at Noah with their bright, inquisitive eyes. There was a pause for a moment, the only sound being the distant bellows of the hippos and the never ending chatter of the monkey families, who never seemed to give up squabbling, arguing and playing amongst themselves. Noah remembered how Duma dreaded them coming anywhere near his nest, as they loved nothing better than to steal eggs and sometimes even young birds. Noah wondered what Duma would say, if he could see him now, ensconced as he was, high up a tree being held by two monkeys. He chased this thought from his mind by concentrating on the fact that Gaia had sent him for this very purpose: to meet all the animals of the savannah.

"Well, what would you like me to say?" finally asked Noah.

"How about telling us how you came to save us from the evil poachers," said Nukky.

Noah thought a moment, and then said: "I was sent by Gaia to do whatever I can to help people of the savannah, I was trying to rescue two cheetah cubs who are friends of mine."

"Friends of yours," hissed Nukky. "How could anyone, and especially a mouse, become friends with, of all things, a cheetah? I find that a little hard to believe."

"Well then shut up and let him tell us. He did say that he was sent by Gaia didn't he?" this from Simian, his friend who, by now had taken Noah up and sat him on his lap.

"Yes," said Noah, who, although he would have preferred to stay on the branch, decided not to argue, if Simian wished to show his friendship in this manner. "Yes, Gaia sent me and I have been able to meet all sorts because of her protection. Anyway, as I was saying, I was rescuing the two cheetahs with my friend, Duma, the hoopoe."

"Don't say anymore, just tell us where his nest is!" said Simian. "Tell us, we would love some fresh hoopoe eggs. Tell us, tell us, quickly."

The two monkeys were now so excited that, with Noah grasped in one hand, Nukky jumped from branch to branch, whistling and whooping in a shrill voice with Simian close behind. So noisy were they, that they soon had a following of other young monkeys all shrieking, "Take us to the eggs! Take us to the eggs!"

Noah, grasped tightly in Nukky's paw, could scarcely catch his breath and all he could see was the flash of greenery and sky above, as Nukky sped as though flying from tree to tree, branch to branch. Finally, coming to the edge of the forest, Nukky realized that he had nowhere further to go and so came to a halt on a branch high up overlooking the busy river bank below. There he dangled with a terrified Noah staring down at nothing between him and the rocks along the bank.

"Well," said Nukky, "are you going to take us there or not?" he demanded.

He placed a thoroughly frightened Noah on a branch level with his head and looked demandingly at the tiny mouse. Noah took several deep breaths and for the first time showed anger.

"No, I certainly am not going to take you to my good friend's nest. What do you think I am, a traitor to friendship? Duma has helped me and been there when I needed him. I most certainly would never betray him and what's more, would you please take me back down to earth? I'm not meant to be swinging high above through treetops. So take me down, and now!"

By now the rest of the troop of noisy monkeys had caught up with Nukky and Simian and, not knowing what it was all about, were surprised at the anger in Noah.

"Take him down! Let him go!" cried the voices from several of the group.

Nukky was suddenly very ashamed of himself. He wasn't really a bad monkey, just one who wouldn't think things out before acting on an impulse. That seemed to be the mode of behaviour of all the monkeys, if they saw something they wanted, or thought of a place to go, they immediately sprang into action. They were lightning quick and impulsive, but they really were not bad, just full of mischief.

"I'm sorry," said Nukky contritely and Simian, too, hung his head, embarrassed that they had been so thoughtless. Suddenly brightening, Nukky, forgetting Noah's anger and request to be taken down from the tree, chirped out, "Hey, I know, look below! It's that grumpy old hippo, Hava, remember her, gang? She is always in a bad mood and chases us, whenever we go down to the water to drink. She thinks that she and the other hippos own the whole river."

Noah looked down and, through the leaves and branches, he could see a huge gray, lumbering mass of flesh. He couldn't think when he had seen anything so awkward and ungainly on land, unless it was Sheba the rhino, whom he had met briefly several days before. Noah had seen the hippos in the water before and he knew that, once in the water, they were graceful and at their ease. They could submerge for long periods of time and they ate the water plants that grew along the river bottom. Once out on land, however, they lumbered about, making loud, grumbling noises and yawning, showing their gigantic mouths with several yellowed teeth and huge gaping pink throats. He also knew that these animals were very short tempered and could easily be roused to anger, especially if they had a young one, which this particular hippo seemed to, a miniature version herself snuggled protectively at her side.

Without any more discussion, Nukky swung down, as low as he could, from branch to branch and began taunting the hippo who, up until now, had been quietly minding her own business, calmly munching on some tender grass shoots growing down the river bank. Shrieking, whistling and yelling, the entire band of juvenile monkeys was off in a flash, teasing, shouting insults about her size and taunting the animal about her inability to do anything about it.

Hava snorted and bellowed as loudly as she could and backed her large body about to face these tormentors, who seemed to be all around and on top of her. Suddenly, a hail of hard-shelled seed pods rained down upon the helpless animal and, while they probably couldn't sting her tough hide, they only served to make her angrier and more belligerent. Noah, looking straight down, could see her tonsils, so widely did her mouth open to roar and bellow in her anger and frustration. The band of monkeys had now worked themselves up into a fever pitch and were throwing anything that they could get their hands on.

A large old crocodile slowly rose up out of a screen of river reeds, where it had been hiding, waiting for some unsuspecting dinner to wander by. Now she slid up onto the muddy river bank, frightening off a flock of weaver birds, which had come for an afternoon drink and had stayed to watch the show. And a show it was: monkeys howling and yowling, now being joined by neighbouring families until the trees shook with their noise and antics. The branch, that Noah clung to, was violently shaken by several monkeys jumping on and off it in fits of hysteria and finally, one monkey landed right next to Noah with such a thud, that Noah found himself flying through the air, only to land bang hard on the river mud, right smack between the bellowing hippo and the open jaws of the old crocodile.

He lay there sprawled in the mud for several moments, before he got his mind back and was able to sit up. When he did so, he saw a crocodile slithering toward him from one angle and an enraged mighty hippo about to swipe him up with that gaping mouth of hers from another. Noah had to think quickly and all he could do was to wipe the mud from his mouth and holler, "Gaia" as loudly and as often as he could, but his tiny mouse voice was completely lost in the din caused by the monkeys who had, by now, been joined in their riot by nearby flocks of birds.

The trees shook, the water roiled with hippos swimming to see the ruckus, and Noah was about to end his days in the stomach of either Hava, the hippo, or the old grandmother crocodile, either one not being how he imagined his end. Just as the two animals were about to butt heads in their attempts to get to the mouse first, a tremendous banging followed by shots could be heard over the noise of the animals. The two poachers suddenly strode out of the forest and stood on the riverbank, firing their guns into the air in rapid succession.

This unexpected turn of events brought everything to a very sudden halt. The monkeys hid in amongst the protective leaves of the trees, the startled birds flew off to parts unknown, the crocodile rapidly slid backward into the reeds and lay there, only her two eyes showing above water to take everything in. The hippo, ungainly on land became confused and tried to charge the two men who, upon seeing several tons of flesh hurtling at them, lowered their rifles and began firing in the direction of the oncoming hippo.

Chapter 12

Back Into the Enemy Camp

WHILE ALL THIS CONFUSION was happening so rapidly, Noah felt himself being lifted unceremoniously off the ground by a monkey paw and once again up, up into the protective branches of the trees. Below, Noah watched with horrified eyes as Hava, the hippo, fell to her knees in a volley of gunshot and then roll over onto her side as blood poured from wounds in her mammoth body. The baby hippo stood by her mother's side whimpering in fear, as the two men threw a net around her and, with not a single look backward at what they had done, hustled the terrified baby off in the direction of their camp. For a few moments there was an awed silence as all the animals who remained were stilled by what had happened.

Suddenly, a shriek, followed by a wail the like of which Noah had never heard before, resounded through the silent forest. Simian's mother held her dead son in her arms on the riverbank and cried a grief so terrible that no one could help or control her. Several others from her family helped her away and her cries could be heard for some time amidst the silence that now hung over the river. Noah, frightened and upset beyond words, tried to comfort the stricken Nukky.

"He was my best friend," he sobbed uncontrollably, "he never meant anyone any harm, he was just full of life."

Noah sat on the branch and waited patiently for the sobs to subside and, when Nukky was more in control of himself, he said, "There must be a way that we can stop these poachers once and for all."

"How?" asked Nukky. "We are just dumb animals, who have no purpose other than to provide people like that with target practice or for them to capture and display us like that poor baby hippo."

Noah was surprised at Nukky's words. They showed a depth of feeling, which Noah would not have thought a careless and carefree monkey to have. Noah was silent for a time thinking. Finally, he said, "Raina is to come and pick me up this afternoon after her hunt, if I tell her that I'm going to spend the night here, maybe you and I could go, in the dark, to the poachers' camp just to look around and maybe find some answers to all of this.

Nukky sniffed, wiped his face with his paw and said, "Do you really think we could do anything, a tiny mouse and one small monkey?"

"Well, we'll never know unless we try. I think that it's better than just sitting here feeling sorry for ourselves and anyway, I'd like to see what has become of that young hippo."

Again Nukky said nothing and, in the silence, Noah could hear birds and animals creating the usual noise around the river bank below. He reflected that, in nature, the wounds of tragedy do not take long to heal, as death is a constant presence.

Suddenly, Nukky, with some of his former spirit said, "Okay, let's take a look at their camp tonight. As you say, it's better than just sitting here and I know that Simian would want us to do something daring like that."

When Raina arrived later that afternoon, she was full of good spirits as she had managed a kill, her first since being wounded by those same poachers. When she heard about the events of the day, she said, "Noah, if anyone can do something it will be you, but please, be very careful." Noah reassured her and introduced his new friend, Nukky.

"Any friend of Noah's is a friend of mine," purred the cheetah but Nukky, who waved a paw at her, did not come down from his perch on a low hanging limb of the nearest tree. Raina left with many words of caution for Noah who listened, because he knew that she really cared.

The evening wore on and Nukky showed Noah several different nuts and seeds that could be gathered from the treetops. They were very tasty and Noah enjoyed eating something a little different that his usual grass seeds. When the sun had set, a different group of animals came down to the river to drink and these included a pride of lions who usually spend the hottest part of the day resting in the shade of trees. After the lions, came Sheba and her little one, Noah did not try to reacquaint himself, as the rhino had not been very friendly the first time and even now showed that she was nervous and ill at ease.

"She can sense danger and the presence of humans," whispered Nukky as they watched from a safe distance above. Later, a leopard, its tail waving from side to side, crawled silently out of the undergrowth along the riverbank and, crouched low, took a long drink before disappearing as silently as he had come.

"We monkeys have to be very careful about leopards," said Nukky. "They can climb quickly and quietly and can snatch you when you least expect it."

The moon had risen over the now silent river and the only sound to be heard was the occasional bird as it flew by on some night mission, and the bubbling noise the water made as it flowed over the rocks on the river bottom.

"I think now is the time for us to go," whispered Nukky, "if the men are in the camp, they will be asleep and we can have a good look around."

So, Nukky, with Noah as always firmly holding onto a tuft of fur on his back, began to glide through the trees in the direction that the smell of smoke told them would be the poachers' camp. Noah noticed how much more graceful and silent was Nukky, as he leapt from branch to branch and tree to tree this night. Not at all like the noisy carelessness of the morning.

Soon they arrived at the same tree that Noah and Duma, the hoopoe, had come to several days earlier, when they freed the captive animals. All was silent. Noah noticed that all of the cages, except one, were open and that meant to him that the men had not captured any more animals except the baby hippo that afternoon. The coals from the fire in the center of the clearing smouldered and every once in a while, a log would crack open showing its fiery red interior. All was silent, as the two swooped down from the trees above and began to explore the camp.

The first thing that Noah did was race over to the cage that he thought held the baby hippo and sure enough, when he whispered at the door, there came a whimpering reply, "Please help me, please help me."

Noah thought to himself that he had heard that same plea many times, since he had come to the savannah. "I will help you if I can," he whispered back. "If we can set you free, where will you go?"

"I can go back along the riverbank, there will be others of my family there and they will care for me," came the reply.

Noah marvelled at how self-reliant this poor, motherless baby was, but he said nothing more and beckoned Nukky over and soon, with the help of Nukky's very flexible, human-like paws with their ever-exploring fingers, the bamboo strips that had been used to seal the cage were undone and the baby hippo, who knew instinctively where to find the river, wandered off in search of her family. Noah watched her plump and ungainly little body, as it plodded off into the trees. He hoped that she would be successful, but he could do no more. Now the two animals turned their attention to explore the rest of the camp. They first found a rough shed which, after being opened by Nukky's ever inquisitive fingers, showed them the tools of the hated poachers' trade. Here were rifles, nets, knives, and other assorted instruments used to capture or subdue wild life.

"There's nothing we can do here, I wish we could destroy all of this but I don't know how."

"Let's look around some more," said Nukky and soon the two found themselves in front of the makeshift tent that the men slept in. All they could hear were the snores of two men sound asleep. "Could we pull the tent down on top of them, do you think?" hissed Nukky.

"What good would that do? They would only come after us again and maybe kill us or some other unsuspecting animal," whispered Noah. "No, we've got to find something else that will put a stop to them once and for all."

The two continued their search of the camp and were about to give up, when Noah spotted a small lean-to that they had not noticed in the dark. It was built up alongside the rows of cages and blended right into the surrounding trees.

"Let's look into this shack," he said and once again, Nukky's nimble fingers untied the binding that held the door together and it swung open to reveal, to Noah's wondering eyes, the answer to their problems. Once before, Noah had had to deal with time bombs, when he had to unwire one in a London subway station and, while what was contained here were not bombs, there were barrels of gunpowder, piles of dynamite and several crates marked "HIGH EXPLOSIVES".

Noah did not think that this was the time to explain to Nukky just how it was that he could tell what these materials were. To Nukky, they were just another heap of human belongings and he was quite ready to leave and get back to the safety of treetops before dawn came and woke the poachers. Noah had a different plan for awakening the two sleeping men.

"Don't ask any questions, please," he whispered to Nukky. Just run over to that campfire, and bring back one of those half burnt logs that are still smouldering."

"Are you crazy, what good will that do? Just wake those men up and cause further trouble." Nukky began to leave the shed but Noah, in a voice that commanded, said, "Do as I say, I know what I'm doing. Now! Fast, and no more argument. You want the end of poaching? Well, this might just bring it about."

Nukky, rather abashed by this new tone of command from his mouse friend, moved quickly to obey, and soon he was back at the door to the shed with a small piece of wood that still glowed brightly at its end.

"Good," said Noah, "Now, just set it here on top of this pile of wood shavings used for packing, and we'll be off."

Nukky did as he was told and before the two had scampered back to the safety of the surrounding trees, the shavings had caught fire and were burning merrily. Nukky and Noah had barely returned to the spot on the river bank that they had left earlier, when an explosion rocked the entire forest, waking birds, sleeping monkeys and frightening a host of other animals, some going about their nocturnal business and others curled up in their nighttime homes asleep, until the dawn's early light.

The explosion was followed by a column of smoke and a pillar of fire that could be seen for miles. Even Raina, far off across the plain, was awakened and when she raced to the opening of her lair, she could see smoke and fire brightening the night sky. She knew that it came from the direction of the river bank, where she had left Noah that day and she hoped that, whatever was the cause, her mouse friend would be alright.

The blast from the explosion tore through the forest, flattening small trees and shrubs and bending taller trees almost double. Nukky, with Noah clinging for dear life, held on to a branch and was almost swept away by the force of the blast. When the trees righted themselves and the forest returned to normal, the smell of burning timber began to fill the air.

"What happened back there, what did we do?" asked Nukky breathlessly. "Were we the ones who started this fire? What do we do now?"

Noah, who knew from the beginning just what they had done, said, "Let's get out of these woods, they are sure to go up in smoke, and we'll go with them if we don't make a run for it."

Now the forest was fully awake and birds and monkeys were all rushing away from the oncoming flames. Below, on the ground, the underbrush crackled and rustled with frantic movement of forest dwellers, all anxious to escape.

"Don't you see what we have done?" shouted Nukky over the roar of the approaching flames. "We will have destroyed the homes and livelihood of all these forest folk, including my own family."

"There is no help for it," returned Noah. "If we are to stop the poachers once and for all, then someone has to suffer. I'm sorry but it can't be helped."

Nukky, with Noah on his back, now flew from branch to branch as fast as he could go. The dry trees and underbrush made the fire burn all the more fiercely until it was out of control, consuming the entire strip of forest that lined the river bank. When the flames reached the bank, the last trees flamed, fell, and the fire soon expired, as there was no place else for it to go.

Noah and Nukky soon found a place to stop and catch their breath; it was on a small outcrop much like the one that Raina lived in and it was not far from the edge of the forest. Here they sat and watched as the fire finally died out, leaving nothing but smouldering trunks of trees and the acrid smell of burnt wood. Nukky was still very upset.

"I hope you are pleased with yourself. Look what we've done! It will take years for those trees to grow back and, in the meantime, where will everyone go?"

"I know, you are right, but if you will just listen, I'll try to explain." said Noah.

"Well, it had better be good, imagine, setting fire to everyone's homes like that!"

Noah was very calm and, he understood Nukky's anger, but he began to explain that, when he saw the barrels of explosives and the gunpowder in that shed, an idea had come to him that, if they were to destroy the very power that the poachers had over them, then perhaps they would go away and not come back.

He said, "I knew in an instant, that here was a way to strike back, to hit them where it would do some good. I knew that some of the forest folk would suffer, their homes being lost, I just hope that everyone escaped with their lives. Don't you see, Nukky, the poachers are gone, and now everyone can get on with their lives. They can find new homes and you have to admit that anything is better than having to constantly worry and having to glance over your shoulder to see if poachers are around."

Nukky remained silent and Noah knew that what he had done would remain in Nukky's mind as a terrible act, and not as a way to rid the savannah of the poachers.

"I am truly sorry, Nukky, but you will see that in the long run, it will be for the better, I promise you."

Nukky, who did not ever think in the future, remained unconvinced. "I will take you to near where Raina lives," he said very quietly, "and then I must go back and see what has become of my family.

Without any more words, he set off across the flat land toward Raina's home. Noah, wisely, stayed silent. He knew and understood Nukky's anger and felt that, even though he had lost a friend, the result of this night's work would benefit all. Nukky stopped near the outcrop and Noah got down from his back.

"Thank you, Nukky; I hope that someday you will understand."

Nukky only replied, "It's getting light, I must get off." And with no further words, he turned and ran back in the direction of the river with its now ruined strip of smouldering forest.

Noah watched him sadly. It was too bad, he thought, but the poachers were gone, and that in itself was worth all the unhappiness and misery. Noah made his weary way up the rise to Raina's cave, where he found her waiting anxiously.

"I heard the explosion and saw the smoke and fire," she said, "and I hoped that you would be alright. What happened? Please tell me everything."

Noah, who was overwhelmingly tired, tried his best to explain the events of the past day. He found that even Raina, who usually defended his every action, was slow to see the advantage of the explosion. All she could think of was the homes and lives of those who lived on the banks of the river and in the surrounding forest.

"Well," she finally said, "I guess that you know best Noah, after all, everyone will have to admit that you have been on their side, when it came to the poachers and no one will dare say anything in my presence against you. Now, you look beat, you had better try to have some rest."

So, Noah went to his tiny nest far in the back of the cheetah lair and was asleep almost before he was able to curl up into his usual ball. Raina kept watch outside the lair entrance and, as the dawn began to awake the birds in the trees, in the distance, she could see a line of smoke where the trees along the river had been. In her heart, she felt that what Noah had done was wrong but, because of the unselfish way he had worked to retrieve her two cubs, she would never utter a word except in his defence. Noah had made a powerful friend and she would remain such forever.

CHAPTER 13

Monsoon

D AYS WENT BY. NOAH stayed very close to the lair and spent much time with the two cubs, who were now growing very fast and would soon be going out onto the savannah with their mother to learn the ways of the wild. Already Raina had weaned them and they were eating chunks of meat that she brought home for them.

One day, while watching the two pretend to hunt and attack one another, Noah's ears picked up the sound of far off thunder, a sound that he had not heard since leaving home. Later when Raina returned from her daily hunt, she said, "We had better prepare for wet weather. The rains look as if they will be here tomorrow."

That night was disturbed by the rumble and explosions of thunder. Noah, at one point, climbed out of his little nest, crept past the sleeping Raina and the cubs and peered out of the lair's opening. The inky blackness of the African night, usually lit only by millions of far off stars, was now overcast with billowing, black clouds that climbed way up into the sky, and their tops were lit by the flickering glow of lightning, which would suddenly pierce the clouds and shoot arrows of fiery, white light into the ground below, always accompanied by huge shocks of thunder which would boom and roll down the corridors of air. Then, the whole plain would become bright for an instant, only to be plunged back into blackness in the next moment. Noah watched, fascinated; this display of the coming storm was like so much here in Africa, larger, noisier and more awe inspiring than anything that he had ever witnessed at home.

He sat there, this tiny scrap of mouseness, and soon, his thoughts turned to home. It seemed so long, since he had sat out in the night on Munificent Meadow and listened to the voice of Gaia. Was he finished here? Had he accomplished anything? It was hard to tell. He had done some very good deeds it was true, but surely, Gaia hadn't sent him all this way just to save several animal lives.

The fact that he had alienated many of his friends by his exploding of the poachers' camp, weighed heavily on his heart. Someday, perhaps, they would understand but until then, he would just have to keep to himself and wait until a sign came from Gaia. He decided that, until that sign came, he would stay close to Raina's lair and enjoy her company and that of Duma who was a frequent visitor, taking time from his busy schedule of finding food and keeping his hatchlings full.

The thunder and lightning display continued and then, a soft and gentle breeze blew across the plain, bringing with it a patter of rain, the first rain that the savannah had seen in over a year.

Noah went below and returned to his bed. He curled up and as he did so, he heard, through the now muffled thunder, the increasingly insistent sound of raindrops now falling harder and harder, until they created a ceaseless drumming sound like that of pebbles falling on a hard surface. Noah slept soundly now, knowing that all was right with the world and that this rain was a good thing and would bring life and relief to the parched plain.

The next day, Raina and Noah sat watching, as the unending rain kept on and this, plus the dull and gloomy light from the low-lying cloud cover, cast a depressing spell over everyone. The cubs were listless, not their usual boundless energy and even Raina, several times snapped a reply to a casual remark of Noah's and once swiped a paw at one of the cubs who rolled too closely to where she was resting.

This seemed to go on for days on end and, just as the inhabitants of the lair felt that they could stand no more of the grey, wet weather, the rain stopped just as suddenly as it had begun and the four animals crowded out to the lair entrance to watch the rays of the warming and welcome sun burn off the mists left by the retreating rain clouds. The land lay below them, soggy and saturated and, here and there, small bodies of water reflected the glow of the setting sun.

"Now I can go out and hunt," said Raina, "and you two will accompany me for your very first kill."

The two cubs bounded about in raptures of excitement. They had been cooped up for so long, and now their young bodies needed to stretch and be free to run and dash about using their muscles as had been intended.

CHAPTER 14

Men in Uniforms

DAYS LATER, NOAH AWOKE as usual with the sound of the finch families busy in their treetop lives and he ventured out into the early morning sun. His eyes widened with delight and awe, when he glanced at the far flung savannah. Instead of the yellow and brown color that he had become used to, now it stretched before him, a vivid and emerald green. The grass had sprouted up and was standing tall and waving in the breeze. Here and there were splashes of color as various plants flowered in the hot sun. Herds of animals, antelopes, buffalo, elephants among others, grazed contentedly in the lush greenery.

Later that same day, Raina returned with her two young. They were triumphant, as Raina had made her first kill of the season and the two cubs, now grown twice the size they were when Noah arrived, were overjoyed, as they had witnessed their first chase and successful kill. They were full of enthusiasm and spirits and Raina observed them proudly.

"They will be the future of this savannah," she purred proudly to Noah. "They, and all the other young, are being born, all across the now fruitful and rich plain."

Noah agreed and as they were conversing, a new sound, one never heard before on the savannah, interrupted the afternoon peace. The animals looked upward only to see a giant, bird-like machine, with a whirling propeller on its top, hover not far from where Raina's lair was situated and begin to descend to earth, its huge single wing rotating so fast, that it could barely be seen. This gigantic bird was a human machine called a helicopter and even Noah stood watching in fear and dread, as he had never seen anything like this before.

Across the savannah, herds of antelope fled in wild panic and elephants trumpeted their anger and frustration at this monstrous, noisy bird, which took no notice of them and landed with a bump on the ground near Raina's outcrop.

Raina herded her two inside and remained huddled in fear at what, to her, might be more poachers with even greater and more devious tricks to trap her or her young. This fear was shared across the plain, as various animals protectively edged nearer to their young and cast fearful glances toward the area where the metallic bird had landed. Many an animal wondered if this was a new attack by the poachers and most hid themselves in undergrowth, caves, nests or wherever they could find shelter. Never had the animal world on the plain felt so open and vulnerable. They were very used to attacks from on land, but never before had danger arrived from the air like this.

Noah, much more used to humans than the others, did not run immediately to hide. His inquisitive nature took hold and he remained on the outcrop, watching and waiting, before he made up his mind about the intentions of the newcomers. While Noah had always had plenty to fear from humans, he also knew that not all were evil and had destruction of nature on their minds. Noah always thought of farmer Boaz as one human, who went out of his way to protect and preserve the various animals, both tame and wild, living on his farm.

As Noah watched, he saw several men dressed in uniforms, descend from the metallic bird. These men were joined by others not in uniform, and the latter soon had unpacked tents and, what appeared to be, camping equipment and soon had a small tent city built with a roaring campfire in the centre. The uniformed men seemed to do very little but snap pictures and observe the surrounding savannah through binoculars. They had papers and were constantly writing and then getting together to discuss. Noah also noticed that there were no rifles or nets unloaded along with the other equipment and he found this very unusual and hopeful.

He reported all of this to Raina back in the lair, but she was not convinced, that humans could ever have any but evil plans towards her and all wild animals.

"You believe what you like," she grumbled, "but you have not lived here all of your life, living each day with worry and fear. None of us can remember a day when we could go about the business of our lives without having to think first, are the poachers out, are the farmers going to shoot us if we cross their land? Always we have had these fears, so I'm sorry if I just don't leap out to welcome these newcomers, just because you say that they don't have guns. Men are underhanded and devious; they must have some other plan of attack."

Noah knew better than to argue with someone who had had such a bitter experience with humans and so, he said little more but waited patiently until evening arrived, and he could see that the humans were finished roaming about the savannah with their cameras and notebooks and were having, what looked to be, an evening meal. He knew enough about humans to know that, after the meal, they would probably spend some time around the fire relaxing before retiring for the night.

As the evening drew on into night and the plain took on the purplish haze that it always did just as the sun set, Noah set off from Raina's lair in the direction of the camp. He did not mention to her where he was headed, as he felt that it might upset and even anger her. He scurried through the now tall and waving green grasses and on his way, he met other, savannah mice who regarded him oddly and when he spoke a word of greeting, they scurried off, glancing fearfully over their shoulders. Noah realized that his nature natter sounded very strange to them and, as he had no one to introduce him, they would regard him with some fear as being an outsider.

On he went, running in small rushes as mice do when they are in a hurry, and he passed other wild beings out for the evening hunt, one of them being a small cat-like creature that Noah almost ran into headlong.

"Whoa there, mouse," hissed the animal, who was indeed a member of the cat family called a civet cat. It was the size of a regular tame cat, but certainly much more aggressive and it gave chase to Noah, who ran as fast as he could.

He passed the trunk of a small tree and ran up it and out onto a slender branch that, he knew, was too weak to hold the pursuing cat. The gray and black striped animal halted halfway up the trunk, its claws digging into the bark.

"So smart aren't you, silly rodent? Well, I can wait here as long as it takes, so there!" and the cat fixed Noah with a green-eyed stare that never wavered.

Noah was so determined to reach the human camp before complete darkness set in, that he thought he really did not want to waste time mentioning his mission from Gaia and spend the time that it would take to explain all that. So, with a sudden, tremendous leap, he shot through the air and landed luckily on his four paws and was off, racing as fast as his little legs would allow him.

The cat was so taken by surprise that, by the time she had backed down from the tree trunk and got onto ground, she could no longer tell which way the mouse had gone and so she spat, hissed and clawed the earth in anger and frustration.

Meanwhile, Noah, not letting up his speed, discovered himself on the outskirts of the newly made camp. Here the grass had been cut down and the earth trampled to make it packed hard and easier for the humans to walk about. For a tiny mouse, however, it made it more difficult to get about unseen. Noah began to scamper across this open space toward the campfire where the uniformed men now sat, smoking pipes and drinking out of mugs. Every once in a while, the low murmur of their voices would erupt into jolly laughter and then subside into serious sounding discussion.

Noah ached to hear what was being said. Some instinct told him that what was going on might just be for the advantage of all. He seemed to know that these men were gentle and quite harmless, not at all like the poachers that he had encountered. In his overwhelming curiosity, Noah completely forgot any training he had ever received about camouflage or being wary when near humans. His flight from the civet cat had left him breathless and unafraid and so, without any further thought, he ran right out into the middle of the circle of men and stopped stalk-still there; when he realized what a foolish thing he had done. Paralyzed with fear, he just remained where he was, half upright, his little face and bright, inquisitive eyes fixed on the men, waiting to see what they would do.

The men, of whom there were five, were also taken by surprise by the sudden interruption by this small mouse that seemed to regard them in an almost human manner. One man broke the silence by saying, with a chuckle, "Well, well, well. Look whom we have here, the first inhabitant of our new park." The other men laughed and then, to Noah's complete amazement, continued their discussion without any further notice of him!

Noah sat down close by the flickering fire, and was now hidden from view by the logs that surrounded the fire and served as seats for the men to sit on. The conversation was fascinating to him and he was now riveted by what he heard.

"That explosion was the last straw up here in this remote district," said the first man, and the others voiced their agreement.

"We have ignored this area and left it to the poachers to rule and plunder the wildlife resources just as they liked. I don't know how or why that explosion went off, but it made a very loud noise and alerted the authorities, that this was one section of the country that needed cleaning up. I wonder who or what was responsible for setting off the poachers' ammunition store?" said one.

"Whoever it was, deserves a medal," said another.

"You're right, we have left this area alone for much too long and it is high time, that we put a stop to it."

"Poachers are an evil blight and must be stopped at all costs, before we find that there are no animals left. As it is, the elephant herd is down to a very few and, at this rate, won't have enough left to bring in a new generation."

"I agree, and the fault lies, for a large part, with these foolish people, who think that animal parts like elephant tusks, rhino horns and lion livers can give them health and youth."

"What fools they are, the world is losing all of its natural wonders, because a few wealthy, greedy people wish for a cheetah coat or a drink of powdered rhino horn to give them youth."

"Well, that will all stop now, gentlemen, because, as of today, this territory has been declared a protected national park, one that is patrolled by rangers to keep out poachers or any other people, other than those who only want to shoot the animals but, with a camera.

CHAPTER 15

Convincing Raina

NOAH TOOK ALL OF this in with a beating heart full of joy. The conversation went on into the night with the men outlining just how the park would be set up. How ranger stations would be built at different points around the park and staffed with men and women who were devoting their lives to the health and preservation of wildlife. Noah heard about how food and water would be made available in times of drought and how veterinarians would be stationed to help sick or wounded animals. This all sounded so wonderful to Noah's tiny ears, that he could hardly wait to get back to Raina to tell her that her fears, and those of the other animals, would be over, that there were good people among the humans and that finally, they had come to offer peace and a place for the animals to live out their lives, as Gaia had intended.

Noah crept out from under the bushes surrounding the camp. He was spotted again and the men laughed and said, "Go on little mouse, tell all the rest of the animals that they now have nothing to fear forever more."

Noah raced away through the undergrowth and he could hear behind him the good-natured chuckle of laughter that followed this remark. He raced as fast as he could through the grass and underbrush. Several times, he startled hunting snakes and once, he almost ran right into the jaws of a dozing mongoose. Noah shouted a "Sorry I woke you!" and sped off faster than he had ever run before. This time, however, he was not running so much in fear as he was in joy to bring the wonderful news to his friend Raina.

When he reached the lair, he was so out of breath that it took him a while to catch it and to calm down. All he could do was to choke out, "Safety and peace and good humans," and a whole jumble of disconnected words that Raina sat patiently listening to.

"Slow down and give yourself a minute, Noah, you are making no sense. Now slow down and speak up," suggested the cheetah.

Calming himself somewhat, Noah finally was able to get out the news about the park, the rangers, the protection and all else that he had heard around the humans' campfire earlier. After he had finished, he sat back and waited for the happiness and relief he expected from Raina. Instead, she merely grunted and resumed grooming the two cubs.

There was a long silence and finally Noah said, "Well, aren't you excited? Aren't you happy about all this? Just think, no more poachers, no more worry about death or capture by those wicked men. Don't you see?"

There was more silence and Noah, almost in tears at his disappointment in Raina's reaction, shouted in anger, "Don't you see what this means for everyone? You need never worry about your cubs again or fear for your life from men who want to kill you and skin you for your coat."

This last was said so brutally, without regard for Raina's feelings, that she was finally moved to say, "Men are bad, all men, since the dawn of time, are bad and are our enemies. Nothing will ever change and I will never believe anything else."

She hissed this with such anger and pent up hostility toward humans, that Noah suddenly realized, that he would never understand the anger and resentment that thousands of years of persecution of killing, hunting, trapping had stored up inside the head of, not just this animal, but of all wildlife that had suffered for so long at the hands of his humans. Noah shut up then and decided to say no more to his friend. He went outside and sat watching the beautiful dawn, as the ever happy and cheerful finch families in the trees chattered and began their day.

All across the savannah, he could see herds of antelope, the elephants, the buffalos, all going about lives as they had done for centuries, and he felt a sense of contentment that he had never felt before. This was all as it should be and now, it would be protected and preserved. Raina would never understand the motives of humans, no wild animal ever could, but Noah, because of his ability to understand human language, had a window into how they thought and now he knew that they were not all evil or had bad intentions. It probably would take a very long time for the inhabitants of this savannah to realize, if they ever did, that they were protected and safe from harm.

Raina, with the cubs tumbling playfully behind her, appeared from inside the lair. "I'm sorry, Noah, I know you mean well, but I will never trust a human as long as I live."

Noah knew better than to argue and so he said nothing, and this awkward silence was broken by the arrival of Duma, who flew in and landed full of gossip about the doings of other inhabitants of the plain.

"And guess what?" he chirped, "Vashti, the old elephant, told me the most incredible story about how one of their calves was sick and how these men, in a kind of uniform, drove up and captured the sick little one. They thought that the calf was gone for good but, would you believe, several days later, the same men drove to near where the herd was grazing and left the little calf as healthy and full of life as she should be. Vashti says she would never have believed it, if she hadn't seen it with her own eyes. She says that the calf told her that the men were gentle and kind and fed her all sorts of good food and that the only time they hurt her was to jab her with a needle, but she thinks that this is what helped her to get well."

Raina darted a sidelong glance at Noah who did not comment, he thought better than to say, "I told you so." Noah was a smart mouse and knew when to speak and when to hold his tongue, and this was not a time for him to make any comment.

"Humph," said Raina, and changed the subject to something else very quickly. "How are your hatchlings?" she asked. "They must be nearly full grown by now."

"Oh, yes, they are, and they are about to leave the nest and then, I think it will be time for me to think about returning north, as you know, I migrate every year at this time, in order to be north during their spring and summer."

"Well, be sure to drop in and say goodbye before you leave," said Raina. "And now, I must be off to do some hunting and teaching these youngsters how to stalk and chase."

Raina left with the cubs and soon Duma flew off to see to his nest, leaving Noah alone with many thoughts running through his head.

Duma had said he was going to fly north. Could it be time for him to leave also? His time here had been busy and he had accomplished many things, the greatest of which was his being the cause of the explosion, which brought the authorities to this area to create a nature reserve. Noah understood how Gaia worked in mysterious ways to achieve results. He remembered how he had wondered how he could possibly be of any use. Now he knew, and he realized that there may be more tasks ahead for him. It was time to return. He missed his real home and he wondered how Grandpa Ezekiel was, and it suddenly hit him that he was homesick and wanted more than anything to return to Wild Wold Farm and to visit Sparkling Stream and to visit Mrs. Yahoody in Munificent Meadow, where it was always cool and peaceful, not like here, where death was never far away and the heat was sometimes overpowering. These thoughts convinced him that the time had come, and he decided to ask Duma, the next time he came for a visit, if he could return with him.

Chapter 16

Goodbye

S EVERAL WEEKS WENT BY, during which Noah spent a lot of time with Raina and renewed his acquaintances with many of the animals that he had encountered during his visit. He especially made an effort to find Nukky and finally he did, while riding on Raina's back one day along the river bank.

The trees that had burnt in the explosion were beginning to sprout back and many shrubs had taken root and were showing signs of regeneration. The usual animals were at the riverside, elephants, rhinos, and many others bathing or just having a drink, before returning to their lives on the plain. Noah watched and knew in his heart that they were now safer than they had ever been. Nukky, along with several of his family and friends, swung by on the low hanging vines and quickly shot away when spotting Raina. Nukky, however, saw Noah perched on her back and called out a greeting.

"Hello, Noah, good to see you."

Noah felt so happy, as he was very fond of his active and unpredictable friend and hated the way they had parted, in anger and in silence.

"Hello, yourself," called Noah. "How have you been?"

"Wonderful," replied Nukky, "we have found a new home near a humans' camp and, would you believe, they not only do not try to capture or harm us, but they even leave out food for us. Life has never been so good!"

And with that, he and his group were off to tease the old grandmother crocodile, who seldom ever stirred from her place in the shallows where she lay, her unblinking eyes waiting for some unsuspecting prey to happen by. Noah was secretly thrilled. Here was another story of how the new nature park was going to be successful. It looked as if humans were here to protect and save.

Later that same day, as Raina, the cubs and Noah were gazing out across the plain, perched on their rocky outcrop, watching the shadows lengthen, as the coolness of dusk took over from the heat of the day, Duma arrived to say goodbye as he had promised.

"I'm off now, so that I can make some distance during the cool of the night," he said.

"Well goodbye then, and I guess we'll be seeing you next year," said Raina.

There was a pause as Duma looked to Noah for his goodbye, but Noah was silent.

"Aren't you going to wish me a safe trip?" said Duma, "You know it's over many miles and over deserts, mountains and across very wide seas, until I reach my summer home."

"I know," said Noah in a very small voice. There was a long pause and then: "Do you suppose that I could come with you? I promise I wouldn't be any trouble and I would help you when I could and I would be company for you."

"Are you wanting to leave this place?" said Duma.

"Well, not because I haven't been happy here, but I am getting a little homesick and maybe that's a sign that it's time for me to go."

"Why, let me think for a moment. I suppose you could, but it might get very cold." He thought for a moment longer and then said, "But you are very small and you wouldn't weigh much, if you were tucked firmly under my feathers on my back. Sure, come along. You will be great company and I won't get lonely, when I have to stop to rest or feed. We'll see some great sights and it will be fun."

Raina, who had not known of Noah's plan, was, at first, quite upset to think that her little friend, who had come to mean so much to her, would soon be gone, probably forever but after a while, she did understand saying:

"I suppose that you must go. This isn't your real home and, although I wish you could stay, I realize that you must return to your own people. Good luck, my small friend, I will never forget you and all that you have done for me and my family and I will never forget the special times that we have had, just sitting here watching the sun set." With that, she leaned over and, with as gentle a movement as a summer breeze, this large beast, who could have removed Noah from this earth with a flick of her tongue, gave Noah a kiss on the top of his little head.

Noah, choked up with tears and through misty eyes, waved goodbye as he climbed onto Duma's back.

"Goodbye, my little friend, and may Gaia be with you always, "Raina roared, as the two flew higher and higher until Raina and the cubs became just dots on the wide savannah.

Over the plain, Duma flew and below, Noah could see, as from a great distance, all the places that he had been and many of the friends that he had made. He could just make out the patrol truck of the rangers on their daily rounds to protect the park. With this image in his mind, Noah lost sight of the savannah as Duma headed upwards flying into the clouds and heading for the far beyond.